# The Father's Design
# to Bless you

Mary Lozano Rengifo

# Table of Contents

# Introduction

Moses was a prophet and a man of God, with whom we can easily relate. Almost everyone knows how God used him to deliver the people of Israel from Egypt, where Pharaoh oppressed God's people. Moses, led by God, was useful in His hands. God shared His plans with him and gave instructions on how to carry them out. The Father allowed Moses to remain on the mountain with Him for forty days; He also gave him the Tablets of Stone, which we know as the Ten Commandments. Moses, the prophet, had such a close relationship with God that the Creator called him His friend, and they talked like this:

The Promise of God's Presence
King James Version

*Exodus 33:12-19*

*And Moses said unto the LORD, See, thou sayest unto me, Bring up these people: and thou hast not let me know whom thou wilt send with me. Yet thou hast said, I know thee by name, and thou hast also found grace in my sight. Therefore, I pray thee, if I have found grace in thy sight, shew me now thy way, that I may know thee, that I may find grace in thy sight: and consider that this nation is thy people.*

I did not develop a personal relationship with God the Father as a child or even a young adult, although I knew of Him from an early age. When I was forty-six years old, I received Jesus Christ as my Lord and Savior, and since then, I have strived to stay close. I understand that He is not only my Heavenly Father but also my savior and my friend. I have had the opportunity to experience His paternity, His presence, and his transforming power over the last twenty years. No past or present glory compares to the one I have experienced with God the Father, the Son, and the Holy Spirit.

The purpose of this book is to embody how my experiences with the magnificent God changed my life and my destiny. I want to portray how a person, by faith, can develop trust in the Invisible One and establish that, although we don't see Him, this powerful and Almighty Creator is continually present in our lives. God empowers, heals, transforms, and lifts His children to a position of power and authority, and blesses them. The Father starts by giving us identity, healing our wounds, providing inner peace, allowing us to trust ourselves, and giving us a hope-filled future. Just as He did with Moses, I trust that God is with me during this journey to guide my thoughts and the pen He has placed in my hands, as He assured me through a prophetic word.

Colossians 1:15
"He is the image of the invisible God,
the firstborn over all creation."

I express a profound sense of gratitude towards my Creator because He rescued me when I felt hopeless and was consumed by sadness and despair. I thank Him for restoring everything I lost in my life, or so it seemed. In the restoration process, God gave my husband and me a perfect measure of Faith that broke our mental limitations. He assigned tasks that we believed we could not perform. He does it because it is He who equips and trusts us.

Never in my wildest dreams would I have imagined writing a book, but God believed I could and equipped me to do it. My prayer is that every written word comes out of the Father's heart, and I become only the channel through which He speaks to the hearts of the readers. May these teachings and revelations help you develop a yearning to understand His designs and know His will, which is Good, Pleasant, and Perfect, as demonstrated in all of creation.

The Scriptures teach us that God the Father walked with Moses when He sent him to bring the people of Israel out of

Egyptian slavery. We know that He showed His Glory many times and confirmed His presence through miracles, continuous signs, and wonders to His people. In the desert, God walked before them during the day and night. During the day, He led them as a pillar of cloud, and at night, God led His people as a pillar of fire, so that they could advance. His manifestations were designed to make the Israelites understand that He was with them, and while this was so, they would not lack anything.

God's first miracle in the desert was to turn bitter waters into fresh water they could drink, as they were thirsty. These miracles demonstrated not only how much He loves His people, but also that He is an All-powerful and almighty Father. If we have Faith and believe, we will also be able to enjoy all His blessings today and tomorrow. God the Father wants His children to experience all the blessings He has in store for them if only we choose to believe.

Ultimately, I write this book to bear witness to the restoration I have experienced. Today, I enjoy total peace, joy, blessing, prosperity, and health, together with a sense of direction, purpose, and fullness of life. God has prepared the same for those who trust Him and allow Him to work in their lives. I can say with certainty that I have seen The Glory of God manifested in me.

*What is the Glory of God?*

The Scripture, in the book of Ezekiel, tells us that the Glory of God is a visible sign of God's presence. Glory is an external manifestation of an internal and supernatural reality.

*What is the Glory of God?*

Apostle Guillermo Maldonado (my pastor for over twenty years), in addition to being the founder of 'King Jesus International Ministry' and the 'New Wine Apostolic Network,' leads the fastest-growing, multicultural church in the United States. A ministry recognized for witnessing the visible manifestations of God's supernatural power and for moving in the supernatural. In this ministry, we frequently experience the glory of God, and in his book, titled in the same way, he refers to it as follows:

# Chapter 1
# First, He Created the Atmosphere


Jeremiah 32:17 (KJV)

*"Ah, Lord GOD! Behold, thou hast made the heaven and the earth by thy great power and stretched out arm, and there is nothing too hard for thee."*


Habakkuk 2:4 says, "the just shall live by faith". Just, or righteous, is he who holds a right standing before God and lives according to His righteousness. Righteous is he who decides to believe *in* God and believe God Himself - that is, His Word, which is embodied in The Holy Scriptures and, after knowing it, obeys it.

The Bible is a book inspired by God, written approximately 1,600 years ago by various men from different eras, social conditions, and diverse professions. Despite the authors' varied origins, the entire Bible contains the same principles, and no verse contradicts another. Also referred to as the Scriptures, they contain prophecies that, although written many years ago, have been fulfilled. This book includes more than ten thousand promises, all of which are intended to manifest in our lives without requiring any action on our part to receive them, except to have faith in their possibility, lead a life of prayer, and remain obedient. Scriptures have promised, for example, that the Lord loves us unconditionally and that nothing will separate us from His love. Sadly, many people struggle to understand how or why He would love us so unconditionally.

From the first book to the last, the Bible's central theme is God's purpose for humanity and His unconditional, eternal love for them. It is an instruction manual for life, where we learn how, why, and the purpose for which He created the earth and humanity. In its sixty-six books, we also learn humanity's responsibilities and God-given rights toward the Creator and Creation, but above all, it teaches us about the love of God.

On the other hand, the love man knows is temporary, conditional, and is primarily based on emotions and feelings that change from one day to the next. However, *Agape love* differs drastically from the love of humanity because God himself is LOVE. His love forgives all, believes all, suffers all, endures everything, is unconditional, eternal, and man cannot comprehend it.

From the Holy Scriptures, we learn about God's love for Humanity as a whole. How much God the Father loves each person in an intimate and personal manner – *that even the very hairs of your head are numbered* (Matthew 10:30). The Father is so close to us that He knows and understands what we think, what we feel, what we need to be happy, prosperous, and healthy internally and externally. God also teaches what to avoid so we remain wholesome and in good standing with Him. He urges us to love our neighbor as ourselves. Healthy relationships are so meaningful to the Father that Jesus summarized the Ten Commandments in two main parts:

Luke 10:27

*"Thou shalt love the Lord thy God with all thy heart, and with all thy soul, and with all thy strength, and with all thy mind; and thy neighbor as thyself."*

The book of Genesis teaches us about Creation and God as the Creator of Heaven and Earth. In the first chapter, we are made aware that "*the Earth was without form and void and darkness was upon the face of the deep*" (Genesis 1:2), and that in seven days, God established order where there was chaos. As a start, He separated the light from the darkness and said, "Let there be light, and there was light" (Genesis 1:3). He called the light 'day' and the darkness 'night'. Then, He divided the waters which were under the firmament from the waters which were above the firmament, and called it *Heaven 1:6*. Then He gathered the waters under the heavens unto one place, and God called the dry *land* Earth; and the gathering together of the waters he called Seas 1:10.

He established time to govern our days and to serve as signs for seasons, days, and years. He declared the sun to be the greater light and allowed it to rule over the day. The moon was called the lesser light to rule the night. He also created the stars in the heavens to shine on the Earth.

God, by his great power, created the Earth, which was formerly void. God is and has always been there from the beginning. Trinity worked together to restore all things and created a good, habitable atmosphere that was void, dark, and disordered. Then God produced the vegetable kingdom – *herbs that yield seed, whose seed is in itself*- 1:11. Next, He created the animal kingdom – *Let birds fly above the Earth, sea creatures and cattle, creeping things and beasts, each according to its kind."* 1:20. He gave life to Earth and created everything to sustain the man He was about to create and form - in **His Image and Likeness**. This is how God manifested His perfect design for what was to come – which was humanity already conceived in His heart. *Then God saw everything He had made, and indeed it was perfect, and God was pleased! Genesis 1:31*

The Bible is a marvelous book. Once we learn to read it, we love it as honey in our mouth". We appreciate it not only for its literal context but because it expands our knowledge of God the Father's great and marvelous works. Through His written word, we learn God's character, His manifested love, and His perfect design for humanity.

*Jeremiah 29:11*

*"For I know the thoughts that I think toward you, saith the LORD, thoughts of peace, and not of evil, to give you an expected end."*

### *Spiritual Likeness*

Once God created the habitable environment and atmosphere, He planned for the man and woman, whom He had already formed in His heart. He said, *"Let us make man in our image, according to our likeness."* With these declarations, He established the design for humanity who would walk on Earth, starting with Adam. Then, God formed man from the dust on the ground and breathed into his nostrils the breath of life; and man became a living being. The body was designed to perfection. It is the spacesuit with which we all sail on Earth during our natural life. This precious armor contains the essence of the Spirit of God in itself, therefore we should not think of dividing the Body from the Spirit because "know ye not that your body is the temple of the Holy Ghost which is in you, which ye have of God, and ye are not your own?" 1 Corinthians 6:19 (King James Version (KJV)

Each man and woman carries the Father's image, which was imparted through His "Breath of Life." The Father introduces the Holy Spirit in man, thus giving the body a mind with the intellectual and emotional capacity, from which man's will either yields, or does not yield to the Lord.

Just as God is a tripartite entity because He is:

### *Father, Son, and Holy Spirit*

Man is a Tripartite being for possessing:

### *Body, Mind, and Spirit*

God's original design for man was fulfilled when He imparted His Paternity and revealed Himself to His creation. He makes Himself known through an intimate, personal relationship founded on pure and unconditional love for those He loves the most: His children.

By creating man as a tripartite being, God equipped him with the necessary powers to govern and multiply. God also provided in the environment and atmosphere all the resources mankind would require to govern and multiply. As long as man developed and maintained intimacy with Him, the Father would give direction and wise counsel on an ongoing basis. This paternal relationship fosters harmony with the Father, with humanity, and with himself as an individual, all of which reflect a profound sense of peace.

Had man remained within the Father's perfect design, he would have never experienced social injustice, illness, misery, poverty, or brokenness. Nor would he have entered into disputes and divisions with others, nor felt jealousy, malice, or evil, as these are all conditions of a heart void of love and total lack of identity. The Father's design was to be a blessing for all humanity when He created Adam and Eve, the first couple.

The purpose of the Creator has always been to maintain a relationship of communion and intimacy with humanity while expanding His Kingdom and Righteousness on earth. This truth was debated when Adam disobeyed and because of the Original Sin, all humans needed redemption as the world plunged into a state of chaos and disorder.

God's redemptive plan restores the intimate relationship between man and the Father, the Son, and the Holy Spirit, and grants them continuous and unconditional access to God's presence. Let's remember that the Father's design remains valid, and His plans will always prevail.

These concepts are essential because a Godly man is well-educated to manifest his tripartite existence, thereby establishing a healthy, safe, and progressive society that is always in favor of Humanity and not self-interest. A son of God knows that he was born to govern, decree, and establish God's plans because he carries the Power that Jesus gave him as a "blank check, without reservations.

With His declarations, God not only formed man's body but also his purpose for existing on Earth for this appointed season. With His Breath of Life, God created man in His image. He did it in this simple and natural way because we are the visible, living representation of the invisible God in Heaven. As children of the Almighty God, we represent the Kingdom of Heaven on Earth, no matter our condition, origin, race, or nation in which we were born. Each man and woman carries within themselves the fundamental task of manifesting God's Kingdom in their circle of influence. We are clothed in authority, equipped to rule as the visible heads and monarchs in the world of an invisible kingdom, and neither lack strength nor power. This does not mean we will rule over others to oppress them; on the contrary, we must all build, affirm, and bless each other and never oppress anyone.

A recent scientific, modern research came to the irrefutable conclusion, aligned with God's Word, where it declares, *"And hath made of one blood all nations of men for to dwell on all the face of the earth, and hath determined the times before appointed, and the bounds of their habitation."* **Acts 17:26 King James Version.**

It does not matter how much an increasingly small part of the world strives to preach against this. We all come from the same Creator, and the same blood type runs through our veins, regardless of the ethnic group to which we belong.

# Personal Testimony
# My Beginning

I was born in Bogotá, Colombia, in a home where my parents professed to be Catholic more out of tradition than conviction. I am the fourth of the six children my parents conceived. During the first eight years of my life with dad and mom, I grew up like many other children. During the holidays, we traveled as a family, we had fun, went to restaurants, and received much love. On Sundays, we would play with our dad and sit together at the table to share meals. We were all punished and disciplined with love. Like all the children, we played, fought, challenged, and supported one another. The most valuable and significant aspect of my family is that, even today, all siblings remain committed and supportive of one another.

As in most families raised with Catholic religious beliefs, God was sought by tradition, by custom, and without much revelation of what it means to know our Creator. We looked for Him to solve problems in times of crisis and difficulties. I had learned that although almighty, He was also punitive when we failed Him, and that we always did. Either way, we feared and kept away as much as possible to avoid experiencing punishment when we failed. Traditionally, religious holidays and feasts were celebrated by taking trips and making the most of the long weekends to party. We learned the importance of fulfilling the sacraments established by the universal church, such as baptism, confirmation, communion, marriage, and extreme unction for the sick; yet, we had no biblical foundations for any of those practices.

During the Holy Week, our mother gathered her four youngest and asked us to repeat the name of Jesus one thousand times. A traditional, annoying, and infinite rite for us, which consisted of mentioning the name of Jesus a thousand times, mechanically, and without a clear understanding of what we were doing. We did not understand the power of Faith in God, nor the power of prayer from a righteous person.

During moments of crisis, when my parents' marriage was not going well, and they were considering divorce, our mother would gather us to pray repetitively, but without knowledge or understanding. Unfortunately, we were unable to recognize the *spiritual power* God had deposited in each of us at the time of such need, thus failing to use it. As a result, we did not obtain tangible results from our prayers. That is what my parents learned and passed on to their children (instructed in religion, as most of our ancestors were), and so we grew up mistakenly thinking that we were doing something right that did not yield us positive results.

As I grew up with these teachings of prayers without answers, of a Christ who was not alive but crucified and hung on a wall of the house, utterly devoid of spiritual manifestations, this is what I involuntarily and innocently always practiced. Even though I had faith, the size of a mustard seed, I did not expect answers to my prayer requests. I did not develop the ability to "move in the Spirit of God" during my early years. Neither did I understand that I had the right to be called a daughter of God, who possessed spiritual inheritance and was created in His image, and was a carrier of a level of authority and power capable of changing all the adverse circumstances that life presented. I did not have the revelation of what this meant to me or how to use those spiritual weapons. I missed out on the opportunity to learn God's will, seek His presence, and walk through life with His blessing. I now understand that we could have known and allowed God into our lives, hearts, and homes through His love.

In Hosea 4:6, it is stated, "My people perish for lack of knowledge." This means that due to a lack of knowledge, our long and repetitive religious practices did not mold our hearts or connect us with the God of Heaven. I loved God because I learned to love

Him, but not in the way I do now, with a close and intimate relationship. Today, I love my Heavenly Father with all of my body, heart, and mind to the extent that I entirely understand Jesus Christ is alive, real, and the absolute center of my life.

This testimony is relevant and revealing because it genuinely represents realistically the consequences of the Original Sin and the fall of man from the Father's Grace. It is a glaring example of how, over the years, men turned against God or, at best, cold-favored humanism. We have forgotten, if ever we knew, to seek Him to do His will. Frequently, we ask Him to solve our crises, and after He helps us by His mercy, we distance ourselves from Him again. From my family experience, I learned that money was an essential value in life. Thus, before knowing Christ, my God was money. I aspired to have lots of money because I erroneously thought it would be my mark of success and the way to be accepted. Furthermore, I expected it to be the solution to all divine and mundane problems – WRONG ON ALL COUNTS.

In the spiritual sense, the worldly power of money is a spirit called Mammon. During the Middle Ages, Mammon was commonly personified as the demon of greed, wealth, and injustice, a characterization that remains unchanged.

I end this part of my testimony by saying that it is not bad, nor is it a sin to have money - "*The earth is the Lord's and everything in it, the world and all who inhabit it*" (Psalm 24: 1). What displeases God is the 'love of money', which occurs when money becomes an idol, and we misuse it. Instead of blessing others, we become greedy, and our hearts become sinful. In rescuing me, God delivered me from the same thing that happened to the rich young man described in His word:

Luke 18: 18-25

King James Version

*"And a certain ruler asked him, saying, Good Master, what shall I do to inherit eternal life? And Jesus said unto him, Why callest thou me good? None is good, save one, that is, God.*

*Thou knowest the commandments, Do not commit adultery, Do not kill, Do not steal, Do not bear false witness, Honour thy father and thy mother. And he said, All these have I kept from my youth up.*

*Now when Jesus heard these things, he said unto him, Yet lackest thou one thing: sell all that thou hast, and distribute unto the poor, and thou shalt have treasure in Heaven: and come, follow me. And when he heard this, he was very sorrowful: for he was very rich. And when Jesus saw that he was very sorrowful, he said, How hardly shall they that have riches enter into the kingdom of God!*

*For it is easier for a camel to go through a needle's eye, than for a rich man to enter into the kingdom of God.*

That is, not for having wealth but for loving it more than God himself. If this rich young man had believed in Jesus and followed Him, his riches would have multiplied because the God we preach never asks us for anything unless it is to increase it. He well knows that money is necessary to advance the Kingdom. God is not against wealth; However, He condemns the fact that we love money more than we love Him.

# Chapter 2
# God's Design for Man
# The Perfect Plan

Genesis 2:1-2

*"Thus, the heavens and the Earth were finished, and all the host of them.*

*And on the seventh day, God ended his work which he had made; and he rested on the seventh day from all his work which he had made."*

When God saw, contemplated, and analyzed what He had made, He decided *that it was perfect* (Genesis 1:31). The Creator concluded that man would carry out His design. All would be well because He not only created man but also gave them His image and likeness. Therefore, having completed His original intent for Adam – and all humanity in general - everything would be okay because God equipped man from the supernatural dimension, in which the Spirit is the predominant force, to navigate in the natural dimension during his season on Earth. In the Garden of Eden, Adam was king and lord, endowed with creativity, gifts, talents, an incalculable intellectual capacity, and significant meaning for his life. Everything manifested the perfection of God's design. Adam was created as a tripartite being, with a <u>body</u> to navigate the world, <u>a mind</u> (to house his intellectual capacity, <u>a will</u> (to experience different emotions or sensations), and <u>a spirit</u> through which he could connect with God.

### The Spirit:

Our precious Creator used the Breath of Life to impart His Holy Spirit and imprint His seal on humanity. God established our similarity with Him in the Spirit because God is an eternal Spirit who does not have, and therefore does not need, a physical body. Thus, our relationship grows through communion in and with the Spirit, not with the mind or the emotions, even if these are involved when we recognize our need for the Father.

### The Mind:

Job 12:10

King James Version (KJV)

*In whose hands is the soul of every living thing, and the breath of all mankind.*

The book of Deuteronomy 6:5-6 says, "And you shall love the Lord your God with all your heart, and with all your soul, and with all your strength. And these words that I sent you today will be on your heart."

God's will is repeatedly declared in His Word. Furthermore, He offers us a significant number of blessings when we voluntarily decide to make Him Lord of our world, above all other lords or gods there may be. However, He will never force us to do so because God is limited by His Word, which establishes His commitment to honor the Free Will He granted all men. Imagine your children, the ones whom you love and nurture with so much love, honoring and loving friends and neighbors more than they love and honor you. How would you feel?

The 'understanding' is one of the most valuable components in human capital (cognitive ability) because it is where man houses the intellect, the will, and the emotions. However, the mind is not inclined to favor the best relationship with God, as man tends to reason everything. Duality or confusion arises when we fail to understand that it is not reason, but faith —that is, believing without seeing —what is necessary to produce the expected results. "Without *faith*, it is impossible to please God" (Hebrews 11: 6). But not only do we not please God without faith; we will not see his manifested work either because "... by faith and patience, the promises are inherited" (Hebrews 6:12).

Why can't we relate to God exclusively through the mind? Because of its very design. The mind and the body were designed by God, as necessary elements for man to navigate this world during his time on Earth. With the mind, man governs the realization of his plans and steps. Through the intellect, man learns, understands, makes assumptions, develops, and deals with the complexities of life. With the mind, man subordinates all his experiences to understanding. Despite this, it is essential to recognize that spiritual things cannot be discerned except with and by the Spirit. To make Himself known, God gave us faith.


*The Will:*

The *will* and *intelligence* are the marks of human existence. The ability to exercise our free will is proof that humans have the freedom to decide for themselves. In most ways, the will is linked to social behavior and involves our sense of morality and responsibility, reflecting and affecting the individual's actions. Although somewhat complex to define and conceptualize, one of the goals of this book is to show how our beliefs about 'Free Will' operate and impact our sense of independence and the consequences of our actions. A person without God uses his will to do what he thinks best for himself, with a marked sense of independence from God and even others. He lives trying to achieve the best for his own "ego," often at the detriment of others.

In turn, God, as the good Father that He is, manifests His will to his children, which is good, pleasant, and perfect. He teaches the value and importance of interdependence- and how much we need, both from God and from each other – although He never imposes Himself, because He respects our Free Will, just as He established in His Word. The will is powerful, primarily when used to fulfill the purpose the Father has placed in him, through His Spirit. In the world and outside the Father, man intends to pursue what makes him feel good and what seems profitable for himself, all based on his own opinion, because he refuses to consider or acknowledge God's thoughts for him.

My heart was transformed when I learned what God spoke through the prophet Jeremiah in Chapter 29, Verse 11: *"For I know the thoughts I think toward you, saith the Lord, thoughts of peace, and not evil, to give you the end you expect."* If God is thinking of me, I certainly want to know what those good thoughts are, because in my experience, when I did things my way, I was wrong many times and did not achieve the end I expected - often, I only got disastrous results.

After they ate the fruit of the tree of knowledge of good and evil, humanity has been trying to cover up its independent nature, not with leaves but with achievements and successes attributed to itself, thus taking all glory and honor due to the Creator. It is a blessing to understand that we primarily need to depend on God and recognize Him in all ways because His hand is the one that blesses us.

*The Emotions:*

We can define emotions as very subjective and complex internal experiences that affect a person's mental state. It is to these emotions that we have given the cognitive value we assign to love, anger, anxiety, and fear, among many others. We tend to navigate our world with emotions, although it doesn't have to be that way. Nonetheless, emotions influence our well-being and also have the power to positively or negatively affect our most mundane or routine thoughts, as well as the most profound ones.

Research shows that 84% of our thoughts tend to be negative and seriously affect our mood, resulting in depression, anxiety, anger, low self-esteem, and many other troubles. Emotions involve the sensory, physical, and social state used to help man react to fear, joy, love, sadness, pleasure, or anger, among many others. However, we should not allow our emotions to dictate our behavior but rather control them to avoid those negative or super positive behaviors, which can deter us from reality by marking disadvantageous ups and downs in our responses. Primarily, the pattern of how we experience emotions results from our beliefs and the values we hold in life, as well as the priorities we have established based on the principles developed within our family and society.

At all costs, men want to feel good and have pleasure, and avoid suffering, sacrifice, or surrendering their will. Through emotions, man seeks to escape or numb pain. He resists with all his strength to go after God and develop the type of relationship God wants us to have: The Father in control and man submissive in obedience, doing His will. From the Word of God, we learn that all emotions are important and valid; God has given us the ability to experience them, although we strive to subordinate them to the spiritual.

Let's see how the Scriptures validate and accept emotions:

- The fear described in Psalm 34:4: *"I sought the Lord, and he heard me, and delivered me from all my fears."*

- The joy described in Psalm 37:4: *"Delight yourself in the Lord and he will grant you the desires of your heart."*

- The anger described in Psalm 37:8: *"Leave the anger and forsake the wrath: fret not thyself in any wise to do evil."*

- The affection described in Romans 12:10: *"Loving one another with brotherly love; as for honor, preferring each other."*

Although our emotions indeed reveal what we love, what we hate, what we trust, and what our fears are, in the end, we cannot bend our most important decisions to those emotions, because, among other things, these fluctuate often and are often very misleading.

Proper education and meditation on the Scriptures and communion with the Father develop the intellect, without giving rise to doubts or reasoning. We cannot understand the things of the Spirit through logic.

Our being – body, mind, and will- must always be subject to and obedient to the direction of the Spirit of God already within us. All humans are a 'spirit' – eternal beings. What happened is that we became accustomed to the natural, relying mainly on our senses (what we see, hear, smell, feel, and touch), and for this reason, our 'Spiritual Being' remains underdeveloped and dormant. However, when we surrender our lives to Jesus, we are revived because the Spirit of God comes to dwell in us. He comes to guide us into all truth and make us a Temple for God, and from this place, we surrender our will and offer a continuous sacrifice that rises to His presence.

**Romans 12:2**

*"And be not conformed to this world: but be ye transformed by the renewing of your mind, that ye may prove what is that good, and acceptable, and perfect, will of God."*

This transformation is a process that takes time, discipline, perseverance, faith, unity with the Holy Spirit, and much dedication. One of the obstacles we face is that we live in a society that seeks instant results in all activities. We have not learned to recognize the benefit reaped from qualities and character developed as a result of bearing the fruit of the Spirit: love, joy, peace, faith, goodness, long suffering, gentleness, meekness, and temperance: against such, there is no law. Once we learn to bear this fruit, if we live in the Spirit, let us also walk in the Spirit and manifest the qualities of our Christ-like Walk, because these will be grounded in the Lord God Himself and His nature and character.

*The Body:*

The body is composed of eleven incredible systems that keep us healthy, vibrant, and functional. The body is perfectly designed to be the spacesuit that navigates Earth during our natural life. Although it is holy, because it contains the essence of the Spirit of God, we should not think that we can divorce *the body from the Spirit* as if *the Spirit* were the only thing that matters. Our body is a powerful masterpiece. So much so that science still does not fully understand its beautiful complexities.

Psalm 139:13-16
New King James Version (NKJV)


*For You formed my inward parts; You covered me in my mother's womb. I will praise You, for I am fearfully and wonderfully made; Marvelous are Your works, And that my soul knows very well.*

*My frame was not hidden from You, When I was made in secret, And skillfully wrought in the lowest parts of the Earth.*

*Your eyes saw my substance, being yet unformed. And in your book they all were written, the days fashioned for me, when as yet there were none of them.*

Our life is not an accident, nor is it a mistake made by our parents. The Father was present, very carefully forming each of the body parts and cells to give us life. He used our parents to bring us into the world when our time to walk on Earth came, so we could manifest the Father's Design for us. It is a design introduced into our Spirit, like a seed. When we are born, we bear this seed of purpose, and in due time, if we have discovered it, we manifest and bear much fruit with it, always blessing others.

1 Corinthians 6:19
New King James Version (NKJV)

*Or do you not know that your body is the temple of the Holy Spirit in you, whom you have from God, and you are not your own?*

*The Original Design for Man*:

Upon receiving God's image, a man neither possesses nor knows evil, has no sin, and has no condemnation in him. So much value is assigned to mankind that the Father gave him the power to be called 'Son.' When He created us, he intended to have a relationship with the Human Family that he planted on Earth. God longs to be able to manifest His fatherhood to His children, to nurture, guide, and love them from His Spiritual Essence. The main legacy of His relationship with men denotes a compelling and inexorable love story, which He decided to bestow upon every man and woman walking on Earth. This gift is intimate, personal, and, as far as He is concerned, it does not change or have any conditions.

Apostol Guillermo Maldonado, in his book, "I Need a Father", said it clearly:

*"He knew that in life, fatherhood was not an option but a necessity among men - and he gave it to us."*

Psalm 139:1-6

God's Perfect Knowledge of Man

*"O LORD, You have searched me and known me*

*You know my sitting down and my rising up;*

*You understand my thought afar off.*

*You comprehend my path and my lying down,*

*And are acquainted with all my ways.  For there is not a word on my tongue,*

*But behold, O LORD, You know it altogether.*

*You have hedged me behind and before,*

*And laid Your hand upon me.*

*Such knowledge is too wonderful for me;*

*It is high, I cannot attain it."*

*God reveals Himself by His Word:*

Every book from Genesis to Revelation embodies the essence of what God wants to reveal. We might think that before creating the world, God lived only in Heaven. Once He formed and set order on the Earth, His design was to establish and expand His Kingdom with His earthly family. Every kingdom is composed of a king, a kingdom, the citizens, and the territory the king governs. In the Kingdom of God, Jesus Christ is the King who rules from above; the children are the citizens who follow Him. God appointed His children to be the kings and priests who govern with authority over the assigned territory. The priests minister the heart of the Father to the people with truth and integrity. The task is to know Him intimately and personally, so that we can impart to others what we know, see, and experience with Him. All united, we must conquer and occupy the territory that has been given to us to possess, together with Christ. In the previous chapter, we saw that initially, all authority on Earth was given to Adam. However, when he disobeyed God, Satan took the keys of power and authority over the Earth for a specific period.

Even though the Creator designed humankind to reflect His heart and rule over the Earth and expand the kingdom, Adam fell from grace. His act of disobedience brought corruption and caused God's design to be lost, but not forever. Consequently, death and suffering entered the world. Adam and Eve became aware of their nakedness and lost their perfection and sense of righteousness. They fell from a state of innocence and lost the fellowship they enjoyed with the Father. Their sin brought about the curse against the ground, resulting in troublesome thorns and thistles, as well as a change in the way the natural world operates. The land inside the Garden of Eden and throughout the whole Earth was cursed. Physical death came to all humanity. Their eyes were opened to make them aware of their nakedness, to feel shame, and a desire to cover up. To do so, they tried to sew fig leaves together, but since those efforts were vain, God himself clothed Adam and Eve. God understood they could no longer walk before him in innocence. God's clothing on them serves as a reminder that our salvation does not come to us through works but by grace when He clothes us in His righteousness.

Romans 3:16-18
New King James Version (NKJV)

*"Destruction and misery are in their ways;*

*And the way of peace they have not known.*

*"There is no fear of God before their eyes."*

Since then, all humanity has leaned toward sin. There is deception in the heart, and man is desperately ill physically, mentally, emotionally, and spiritually. Man's polluted nature silenced the *Spirit* that God placed in him. We have all settled for the humanism preached in society and see no problem normalizing what is sinful. We call the good bad and the evil good, excusing this sinful attitude as a case of "human nature," disregarding and often deliberately ignoring that we are called to rise above all evil doings, by the Spirit of God within us, in our *spirit*.

In our strength, it is impossible to overcome our sinful nature. Alone, we cannot resist our flesh, temptations, the world, nor the devil. God created man to live in His presence through the Holy Spirit, who dwells in those who invite Him in and yield their will to Him. Without Christ, we are and will be victims of our weaknesses. Sin makes us slaves and deceives us, making us think that we are free to do what we want and choose to do. We believe and promote the idea that everything we do is thanks to the *freedom* given, but the truth is that without Christ, we are slaves to the sin that hunts us.

These sins include alcoholism, drug addiction, idolatry of people, and vainly professing love for money, possessions, and deceitfulness. Pride, vanity, gluttony, not just for food but for all types of excesses, lying, loving work more than God, play, entertainment, misguided sexuality, fornication, lasciviousness, and lust for things that we love more than we love the Father. The Father is quite clear and knows we have these weaknesses, and that is why He is so merciful and compassionate. He understands the weaknesses of the flesh and gives us the strength to overcome, but in the end, He cannot and will not be mocked.

The Scriptures teach what man is to believe concerning God and what God requires of him. The Scriptures are a shadow and a sign of the three in the Trinity – *the Father, the Son, and the Holy Spirit*. In an orderly manner, each member of the Trinity exercises God's purpose for His creation, redemption, and administration of mankind. There is not even a single comma in the Scriptures that does not carry a powerful and implicit message in itself. These messages are known as the Rhema Word.

The rhema word is more profound than the logos, or the general word to the naked eye. I researched the four rivers that flowed to water the Garden of Eden and the materials they contained to gain a deeper understanding of what God is saying in the Word, because when we align with His will, we comprehend the Word of God. Here is what I found:

*Genesis 2:10-14*

*"And a river went out of Eden to water the garden, and from thence it was parted, and became into four heads.*

*The name of the first is Pison: that is it which compasseth the whole land of Havilah, where there is gold;*

*And the gold of that land is good: there are Bdellium and the onyx stone.*

*And the name of the second river is Gihon: the same is it that compasseth the whole land of Ethiopia.*

*And the name of the third river is Hiddekel: that is it which goeth toward the east of Assyria. And the fourth river is the Euphrates.*

*Gihon* means waterfall or waterfall that descends from top to bottom with much noise. This concept is related to that of the Baptism in the *Holy Spirit,* which comes and covers us with power from top to bottom.

*Hiddekel* means flowing in its channel, fast waters. When it descends and runs through the valley, there is much fruit, the product of the abundant streams that flow. Applied to our life, it relates to the fruit of the Holy Spirit. The fruit is the character of Christ formed in ours *(Psalm 1:3; 65:9-13; John 15:1-5; Ezekiel 47:12).*

*The Euphrates* means copious, abundant, or profound, representing our eternal house where there will be no more suffering, sickness, scarcity, death, sin, or darkness. We will be with Jesus forever, enjoying the dwelling he has prepared for us *(John 14:1-3; Ezekiel 47:3-5)*.

These waters contained valuable materials related to what the Father prepared in advance for our Spiritual Path. Gold represents the divine nature we receive when we believe in the Lord Jesus, and in the work He performs in those who give him the legal right to enter their hearts to purify and transform their minds. Despite this, we still have many impurities in our way of thinking. For that reason, every time we act according to our natural being, against God's will, we feel an intense sense of contrition that leads to repentance. Inner suffering is a purification process that is needed to transform our minds. The Apostle Paul, author of the book of Romans, urges us to undergo a metamorphosis, likening it to a similar process where fire is needed to refine gold.

The Apostle Peter makes the same comparison saying: "In this you greatly rejoice, though now for a little while, if need be, you have been grieved by various trials, that the genuineness of your faith, being much more precious than the gold that perishes, though it is tested by fire, may be found to praise, honor and glory at the revelation of Jesus Christ." (1 Peter 1:6-7).

The various trials God has for us are opportunities where we can throw our impure thoughts and actions into the fire of the Spirit. In addition to the gold from the land of Havila, where the Pison River passes, there is also Bdellium, a kind of plant pearl, resulting from the abundant sap that breaks the bark of certain trees. "It works as a hammer that breaks the hardened stone of our hearts."

The Bdellium represents the work of the Son and manifests the eternal and constant presence of the Savior before it became necessary for man to require redemption. This presence remains throughout the salvation, deliverance, and healing process. The Word says that when God delivered and brought his people out of Egypt's slavery, he fed them with manna in the desert.

The Spirit of God is always present and continually working in us—mind, heart, and spirit —to make us useful silver utensils in the construction of His temple, the Church of Jesus Christ. The groom, Jesus Christ, comes to look for his bride, the church, and wants to find her without spot or wrinkle, without sin or evil. You and I, beloved reader, are the Church of Christ.

When a grain of sand enters the oyster, causing friction, it spontaneously produces a secretion to wrap the grain, thereby creating less friction. This process, slow and painful, ultimately transforms the grain of sand into a beautiful pearl. This process is similar to the Lord's work when He died on the cross for each of us, to redeem us and produce the church (the Body of Christ).

Revelation 21:21 says, "The twelve doors were twelve pearls; each of the doors was a pearl. And the city street was pure gold, transparent as glass." These doors, which are the entrances to the holy city, are the result of the suffering of Christ, who loved us without measure and gave Himself for us.

In the land of Havila that surrounds the Pison River, precious onyx stone is found. The Onyx is red and represents the blood that Christ shed on the cross. With the blood He shed, He paid the full price of buying us eternal life. We can see the precious stones at the end of the New Testament, in the New Jerusalem, whose brightness will be similar to a stone-like jasper, diaphanous like crystal. The foundations of the New Jerusalem wall are adorned with all kinds of precious stones (Revelation 21:11, 19-20). Each stone has a color that represents a characteristic of God's work in us. The color red refers to redemption. The green color of life and the variation of its hue represent the different levels of spiritual maturity. For example, in plant life, when a plant begins to sprout, it is light green; however, as it grows, this green becomes darker, intensifying in color. Among the twelve precious stones, there are three different shades of green; the most intense is the jasper stone, representing the maturity of life.

Silver is present in the building of the tabernacle in the Old Testament and represents Christ's redemption (Exodus 26:19-25; 30:12-16). In the New Testament, the Apostle Paul speaks of silver in the church building, implying that the church is not a physical building, but rather the people who comprise it (Canaan Ministries).

We see this through the Word that it is essential to God the Father, that His children on Earth feel loved, and that their spiritual walk leads to a constant transformation and purification process of the mind. While it is true that Adam was created perfect, the Father knew what was to come, and the provision to redeem mankind was already prepared. The redemption plan has been in operation since Adam was placed in the Garden of Eden, even before he sinned and fell from *His grace*. Thanks to God's Omniscience and mercy, mankind's past, present, and future sins are all forgiven. The only thing humans have to do is repent and ask for forgiveness with a contrite heart.

The initial representative of humanity, Adam, was created to live in intimacy and communion with the Father because in that type of relationship, he could discover the Father's character, understand His infinite love, learn His purpose, and remain in holiness, enjoying fatherhood. This closeness generates a movement in the supernatural dimension, defined as "a power that enables us to be who He has called us to be and do the things we are called to do."

Unfortunately, due to a lack of understanding of these concepts, we live in a world of orphans today. Due to fatherlessness, men and women walk through life without identity, emotionally wounded and in pain, broken and experiencing a sense of loss and abandonment. Although equipped with all the powerful resources to overcome the challenges that daily life presents, we often struggle to recognize who we are, what we possess, what we represent, and why we are on this planet.

Unlike plants that have a specific cycle of growth, reproduction, and death, God created each human being to transcend and bless others. The Father imparts His blessings through mankind. The problem is that man lacks identity and knowledge; many die without discovering their purpose and go through their lives wandering, fulfilling tasks that were not assigned to them by the Father. They end up dying dissatisfied, without understanding why and with what purpose they walked on Earth.

All the Lord's plans have a *design*, time, and a *process*. When we are born again, the process starts by restoring our broken hearts and healing our wounds. Jesus finds us without identity, lacking *divine paternity*, and often in a state of crisis. The Father embraces us and initiates a process of restoration and redemption that develops our identity in Christ and is vital to our spiritual formation, shaping who we are and where we are going.

**Personal Testimony**

*My life without God*

I was nine years old when my parents' marriage went into a crisis, and ten years old when they divorced. Shortly after their separation, my mother decided to leave Colombia and move to the United States. She asked our father and a judge to authorize our departure from the country and settle in the United States. With a resident visa in her hand, she began our transfer. First, she traveled by herself to get to know the country, learn English, buy a house, and secure a job. While she was consolidating her stay in the United States, she divided her children among her sisters and brothers, since there were too many to leave with just one family. The four youngest children remained in the house of a wealthy uncle, who could take care of us.

By that time, our father had formed a new family and left us. By signing the permits authorizing our departure from the country, he resigned and gave up not only his responsibility to his six children but also the privilege of watching them grow up. For many years, he forgot about us, and we saw him about seven years later. He never accepted responsibility for abandoning his home, his family, or his children. Although I had enjoyed his presence in my early years, I did not have it during the most challenging times of my life. Neither did any of my five siblings.

In the United States, we grew and matured quickly. Each child assumed a responsibility and fulfilled it as necessary for the family's well-being. The oldest was fourteen years old, and the youngest three. Each child processed this change based on their level of maturity and learned to live with the consequences that would mark not only his/her life but also future generations. Each one would have to try to heal the lasting scars on their heart that would define the style of all relationships and many of the assumed attitudes.

When a man decides to leave his wife and home, not only does the husband leave, but the father and provider of the children also depart, and the potential for fatherhood is lost. He goes, leaving them to their luck, thus changing the destiny of each one. That day also changes the emotional, intellectual, mental, spiritual, and economic status of women and children, who remain stunned without understanding the event of abandonment that will forever mark their destinies.

Abandonment, especially if it's a parent's, is one of the most painful wounds to heal. Children marked by abandonment and rejection develop insecurity and low self-esteem, among many other conditions of the soul and weaknesses in personality development. Without the necessary psychological and physical protection of a father, one learns to internalize fear and develop a sense of toxic shame that results from the pain of being abandoned. This is the pain from which people need to heal. It will manifest in the form of anger, rebellion, rejection, distrust for authority figures, and a sense of independence, among others. Since the child's identity has not developed, they will seek acceptance through titles, achievements, and possessions. Even so, the individual will have to deal with the difficulty or inability to relate to others, as they believe that no one can be trusted. The train of thought is that if not even their father could love them enough to remain constant in their lives, how would they dare think someone else will? Abandoned children believe that the fault must be theirs, not the father's.

All children depend entirely on their caregivers to provide a healthy and safe environment in which they can grow up. When this does not happen, they believe that the world is not secure, that no one can be trusted, and that they do not deserve positive attention or adequate care.

While our mother learned to live in the United States, the children in Colombia had experiences that would mark our destiny and break our hearts forever. Our mother did not have a reason or a manner with which to imagine how the people she assigned the delicate and challenging task of caring for four of her six children would act—the four youngest children at that. The relatives who assumed responsibility were parents of an adult son and eight grandchildren. This marriage had the means and enough space to sustain us for as long as necessary. What harm could they, who so kindly offered themselves for this challenging task, do?

However, for a little less than two years, my brothers and I endured conditions of physical and emotional abuse one would never have imagined. Our uncle provided the economic resources for all our material needs. However, he kept himself distant from all eventualities related to our care and the discipline we received in his house. He surely didn't know and was not aware of what was happening to us. I don't remember having much contact with him during that time. As a businessman, he was deeply involved in his investments and allowed his wife to manage the daily routine of his new guests. All this sounds great, except for the methods she used to do it.

Our aunt established a very rigid discipline, which we had to comply with; otherwise, she would severely punish us. The punishment consisted of corporal beatings imposed on either of the three elder children, nine, ten, and eleven years old. The beatings followed a ritual that started with undressing the child, taking a wet rope, she carefully turned it into a whip of about four or six braids with a knot on the tip. She then dipped the whip in cold water and whipped us in the buttocks and back until she felt it was enough, usually until we had black and blue marks from the neck to the bottom of the legs. She hit us in places that would not be very noticeable. I imagine so, she would not have to explain where the bruises had come from. Fearing greater retaliation, no one spoke about what was happening in our daily lives.

Thanks to the fact that we were still small and that we did not carry traces of previous abuse, we were all resilient and survived this painful season of our lives. However, I do not doubt that it left deep footprints in our hearts and marked us in very permanent and negative ways, to the point that they still manifest in our personality and the way we deal with our lives. Our two older brothers and our mother knew about the abuse several years later, when we had already left the "generous" care our uncle and aunt had given us.

Finally, in May 1963, five of the six children traveled to the United States to meet our mother in Miami. A family friend, a pilot, transported us in a cargo plane full of boxes containing live turtles. One of our aunts packed a box of fried chicken to share on the flight, and we were delighted; we left for the distant land that watched us grow. We settled in Miami, where our mother had bought, along with the relatives who had taken care of us, a beautiful house. Being half-owners of the house where we lived, they often visited, and the issue of physical and emotional abuse was never mentioned, so as not to "offend anyone." What was not clearly understood or considered at that time was the emotional damage done to children experiencing this type of abuse. Thanks to God and the advances of psychological studies, this is clear in our society and is addressed and remedied as it should be – most of the time.

In Miami, the attitudes of the family members who had taken care of us changed. The aunt who had been stiff and disciplinary was now kind and acted as if the punishments she imposed on us in Colombia had never happened. We followed that current out of ignorance or fear; I'm not sure. The uncle who had been indifferent and lived busy, now at night, visited his two nieces to molest us sexually, bothering us with sexual advances and inappropriate touches. Our mother, who believed us when we told her, depended too much on his financial support to scare him away, so she chose to ask our older brother to sleep in our room and stay vigilant. The uncle died a few years later without having to face any consequences. The aunt died two or three decades later, alone and in a nursing home. She had lost her vast fortune and ended up penniless after having everything. Her life ended stripped entirely of any affectionate care from the family. The silence we had maintained broke decades later.

When a father leaves his home, he leaves his children unprotected and at the mercy of others. Nobody knows how they are going to treat the children that others take in. Understanding this and based on my personal experiences, I always tell adults who are thinking of leaving their home and their children that nobody will love or care for their children, whether male or female, better than themselves. No one!

The family reunited in Miami, but finding a job proved difficult, so in 1965, we all moved to New York. Alvaro left first, the second-born brother, who was seventeen years old at the time. In New York, he found a job, secured housing, and we all headed north. Alvaro became the protector and the provider of the family at that young age. Needing support, our mother delegated a tremendous amount of responsibility to him. God gave him the strength to bear the enormous burden, and we were all able to move forward, grow, mature, and take on our responsibilities. As our faithful Heavenly Father does not keep anything for himself, he blessed Alvaro in many ways.

In New York, we immersed ourselves in American life. The youngest ones dedicated themselves to studying and taking care of household chores, while the older ones and our mother worked and studied. Ultimately, we all became productive professionals in society. Each one of us is married, has created a family, and has given our best to avoid repeating history. We always stood firm in the intention to never abandon our children, and we succeeded. The American dream was fulfilled, although not without pain and anguish. For us, this was a process of perseverance without faltering or looking back.

I understand the high price paid to achieve what we longed for. In the emotional aspect, no one was allowed luxury or the right to sit down to lick their wounds. With due reason, our mother gave no respite for regrets or sorrows. In our family, there was no place for tears. Although I understand that this left the consequences that we have had to deal with, we thank her because we did not grow up like victims but as fighters capable of facing and overcoming life's adversities, without falling apart.

The tremendous responsibility of raising us well filled our mother with fears. Fear that we would choose the wrong path, develop bad habits, use drugs, or befriend lousy company, all caused her to become rigid, very disciplinarian, and controlling. Her struggle to raise six children well and make each one a successful individual while providing for them financially was undeniable. As a result, we all chose to get married as soon as possible to leave the house and her control, although we all remained close and helped support her until she passed.

In my personal part of this, I married at the age of nineteen to a twenty-four-year-old young man I had known for less than six months. Three years later, we had a baby girl, and in that marriage, I remained for twenty years. Our daughter was and continues to be the most precious gift God has given me. Unfortunately, my relationship with my husband deteriorated, and we ended up divorcing. Over time, we both understood that all we had suffered was because we did not know God. God restores wounded hearts and repairs broken relationships, but we did not know enough to give him the opportunity. Today, we realize that if God had been in our lives as Lord and Savior, we would not have divorced; however, at that time, sadly, we did not understand this.

Jeremiah 2:13

*"Because two evils my people have done. they left me,
source of living water, and they dug cisterns for themselves,
broken cisterns that do not hold water."*

In a natural sense, everything seems to indicate that there is
no reason to bring these past experiences to light. Secrets hidden in
our hearts for well over forty or fifty years have remained silent.
One might even think that time has erased these memories. But it is
no coincidence that there is a movement in the United States and the
world known as "Me Too."

This social movement, led mostly by abused women,
denounces all those who, in the exercise of their ill-founded
"power," have mistreated and abused other people, mainly women
and vulnerable children. They have done it, and they continue to do
so by believing themselves immune to the law. Unfortunately, the
whole world has become complicit in this abuse, allowing it and/or
promoting it through silence. At best, they are silencing the victims
with money. It is time to end all types and levels of abuse, ill-
treatment, and abuse of power.

My one great desire and challenge is for the parents of this
generation to understand that children are a sacred gift that we must
protect with our lives, if necessary. Being aware of this
responsibility, people should strive to solve their problems and

challenges, rather than fleeing to other worlds, abandoning their children, and repeating the same history when things become complicated in the new family.

I mentioned earlier that my father abandoned his children and the family he had formed with our mother to start another family, which he also left after a few years to build yet another. Why? Because the problem was not with any of those women he left behind, but with internal and intrinsic issues he needed to address. However, he decided not to deal with those issues or did not have the know-how. In the end, he opted to run away, thinking that elsewhere he would find greener pastures. Because of those decisions, wherever he went, he left a legacy of abandonment, pain, sadness, and a total lack of paternity.

Proverbs 26:2

*"As a wandering sparrow, or as a swallow in flight, thus the curse never comes without cause"*.

I conclude this segment of my testimony, seeking to understand my father, and clarify that everything he did also had its cause. The Word of God says that there is no curse without cause (Proverbs 26:2). He was born to a young couple, and his father passed when he was a child, leaving his young mother widowed. Although his mother remarried, he grew up without a father in a dysfunctional home and experienced a great deal of rejection during his formative years. My understanding is he gave the children he fathered nothing other than his dysfunctionality and total lack of paternity. He covered up very well-becoming an educated and prosperous man, thus being able to accommodate himself in a society that marked him with rejection as a child.

# Chapter 3
# God Institutes Marriage and Family

The tree of life mentioned in the Book of Genesis was a tree that gave life, as its name implies. The life Adam and Eve experienced and enjoyed in the Garden of Eden (also known as the Garden of God and the paradise of pleasure). It was not the same lifestyle we know today. The Father designed paradise as a perfect place with abundant, pleasant, and endless life. The idea was that in that place, Adam, his wife (yet to be known), and their offspring (yet to be born) maintained their residence. However, it would not be so.

Genesis 2:15-17

*"And the LORD God took the man and put him into the Garden of Eden to dress it and to keep. And the LORD God commanded the man, saying, Of every tree of the garden thou mayest freely eat: But of the tree of the knowledge of good and evil, thou shalt not eat of it: for in the day that thou eatest thereof thou shalt surely die."*

The paternal relationship between God, the Father, and Adam undoubtedly intensified, gained quality, and increased in frequency over time. They loved each other. The Father guided him and gave him access to everything created. God had only set one limit, a prohibition: Do not eat from the tree of the knowledge of good and evil (Genesis 2:9.

If they had obeyed the mandate of not eating the fruit from this tree, everything would have been fine. Otherwise, "the day you eat, you will surely die." Compared to everything God gave Adam, the request to refrain from eating from *one* tree seemed simple. Additionally, God had more for Adam because He had established that it was not good for him to be alone and planned to make him an ideal helper:

Genesis 2:21-25

*"And the LORD God caused a deep sleep to fall upon Adam, and he slept: and he took one of his ribs, and closed up the flesh instead thereof; And the rib, which the LORD God had taken from man, made he a woman, and brought her unto the man. And Adam said, This is now bone of my bones, and flesh of my flesh: she shall be called woman because she was taken out of Man. Therefore shall a man leave his Father and his mother, and shall cleave unto his wife: and they shall be one flesh. And they were both naked, the man and his wife, and were not ashamed"*

When God created Adam's companion, he designed marriage and instituted the family. When a man and a woman decide to leave their father and mother to join and become one flesh with the man or woman they will call husband or wife (man and woman), in the eyes of the Lord, they become one flesh, although not a single entity as each one maintained their identify and individuality. God blesses the families of the world because the institution of marriage has a purpose.

Adam must have shared with Eve, his partner, everything *Abba* (word in Hebrew that means Daddy) had instructed him to do. In particular, he had told them that there was a tree from which they could not eat and that their actions would have negative consequences if they disobeyed. This powerful man must have shown his precious female, the beautiful, majestic paradise of abundant provision. Surely they both enjoyed beautiful moments with each other and with the Father. Paradise was not only the residence for Adam and Eve but also God's dwelling. It was a place where God walked. How many times during these walks in the Garden would the Heavenly Father meet with His children to impart the knowledge and wisdom of His essence?

Genesis 3:8

*"And they heard the voice of the LORD God walking in the Garden in the cool of the day"*.

The Father desired that, as a result of their relationship and the knowledge they acquired about His heart and goodwill towards them, the couple would live under the Divine Law to be well, merely because they discerned that this was good, pleasant, and perfect for them, but not because they felt obligated. This decision reflects the understanding that by staying close, God, the Father and Creator, could teach, discipline, and guide them through a paternal relationship. The care received was affirmed by the perfect love known to man. Abba's love is unconditional, unchanging, has purpose, order, direction, is eternal, and non-transactional.

Both here on earth and in heaven, the only way to impart paternity to another is through an intimate, consecrated, and healthy relationship. The relationship needs to be exclusive and mutually committed. As with a natural dad, our relationship with Abba needs to be exclusive, constant, committed, faithful, and sincere. There is no other way.

In our world, when people do not grow up with a father, a spirit of orphanhood and abandonment can develop, preventing them from receiving the unconditional love and paternity that our Heavenly Father wants to impart. In our limited understanding, we fail to reconcile the fact that if our earthly father, of flesh and blood - whom we could see, could not love us (if he had loved me, he would not have abandoned me), how then will He whom we can't even see love me? Without revelation about the importance of fatherhood, it becomes complicated to learn to relate to our Heavenly Father. To begin the healing process, Jesus must be the center of our hearts, so that the healing process can begin.

The transformation process is essential for God's children as it enables them to experience a constant transformation and purification of the soul. As changes take place, God's children begin to feel loved, accepted, and nurtured. The goal is "to reach the stature of the perfect man, who is Jesus Christ." Many try to be like Christ by eliminating a list of sins from their lives, but this is not what makes us like Him. Sanctification is not achieved through imitation or determination because the things of the Spirit are not attained by personal means or methods. According to the Word of God, we should examine ourselves through a spiritual mirror. That is, "contemplating and reflecting the image of Jesus Christ." First, just as a mirror reflects an image, we receive the image of Jesus. It is necessary to keep in mind that the mirror must be clean and uncovered to receive it. Second, we must be looking in the right direction, and there must be enough light to see. We should not look at the circumstances of the world, whatever they may be, but focus solely on Christ. Third, we must be willing not only to receive the image but also to retain it, with our heart set on Jesus. Finally, it must be reflected because it becomes an inherent nature.

2 Corinthians 3:18

New King James Version (NKJV)

"But we all, with unveiled face, beholding as in a mirror the glory of the Lord, are being transformed into the same image from glory to glory, just as by the Spirit of the Lord."

Only God transforms us through the Holy Spirit. All of us who are fathers or mothers can identify with this desire to have our children close, to guide them and teach them the right paths. We strive to develop lasting relationships with our children, so they know they can trust and count on us throughout their lives, unconditionally. The same desires we have for our children are the same model God has for His children, as we learned these lessons from that model.

Even though He has a latent intention in His heart to relate to His Creation and can call mankind His children, God does not interfere in the life of man unless He is given the legal right to do so. He does not even interfere, knowing the path the child has chosen is wrong and not in their best interest. Nonetheless, in His longing to care for His children, He does send us signs to show us the right path to take. However, due to our independent nature, we often either ignore the signs or fail to recognize them. When someone decides to accept Jesus as their Lord and Savior, they must confess their intention to allow Jesus to influence them; without our authorization or legal right, God cannot intervene in our lives. He gave us *Free Will* and honored His Word. Despite His sovereignty over all Creation, He submits to and fulfills His Word, the highest authority on Earth.

*Matthew 24:35*

*"Heaven and earth will pass away, but My words will by no means pass away."*

Suppose a person decides not to recognize Jesus Christ as Lord and Savior (who gave His life on the Cross of Calvary to pay for all the sins of humanity and restore the path to the Father); such a person will not enter eternity in heaven. Spiritually speaking, *we are all eternal beings*, as are the three persons of the Trinity and the devil, Satan. When man's time on Earth is complete, the spirit and soul go to eternity and remain in the kingdom he or she chose to serve - God or the devil, heaven or hell. There is no temporal stage, a season in purgatory for redemption or reincarnation. The Bible does not mention either of the two states. However, Hebrews 9:27 declares: "And as it is appointed unto men once to die, but after this the judgment." The opportunity to make those decisions is given to us here on earth, during man's lifetime.

When a person does NOT enter eternity with God, it is not because the Father did not invite him. It is because the person decided not to partake with Him, the owner of the place with many dwellings prepared for each guest who agrees to attend His feast. *"In my Father's house are many mansions: if it were not so, I would have told you. I go to prepare a place for you, John 14:2"*. One of his children's assignments on earth is: *"And he said unto them, Go ye into all the world, and preach the gospel to every creature."* Mark 16:15.

*2 Peter 3:9*

*"The Lord is not slack concerning his promise, as some men count slackness; but is longsuffering to us-ward, not willing that any should perish, but that all should come to repentance."*

Again, there is no other kingdom, place, or path; only two places where a man can go when he dies. Every person will be held accountable for the decisions and choices they make. Everyone will decide whether they will serve God or serve Satan, his opponent. The decision is personal. Each person believes and acts according to their conscience, which guides us all, with the corresponding consequences.

In this way and exercising Free Will, Adam and Eve disobeyed the Heavenly Father by eating from the tree of the knowledge of Good and Evil. Although Satan instigated Eve, it was Adam who had the role of leader in the Garden and the relationship. It was to him that God later asked for accounts of what he had done and asked the critical question, *Where are you*?

Genesis 3:9-11

*" Then the Lord God called to Adam and said to Him:*

**Where are You?**

*So He said: I heard your voice in the Garden, and was afraid because I was naked, and hid.*

*And He said:*

*Who told you that you were naked?*

*¿Have you eaten from the tree of which I commanded that you should not eat?"*

I would like to imagine the spiritual rumble that took place when the "Omniscient" asked Adam, "Where are you?" The question had more to do with the condition of their heart than an interest in knowing where they were hidden.

Also, God is asking you and I, "**W*here are you*?**" Where is your heart today for the Lord? The Heavenly Father is very interested in knowing if you are busy seeking His presence or entertained in the world, fleeing, deaf to His call, and wandering without precise direction. He is interested because He loves and yearns for no one to get lost.

John 3:16

"For God so loved the world that He gave His only begotten Son, that whoever believes in Him should not perish but have everlasting life."

*Where are you*? The Father designed this question for us to deepen and meditate within ourselves. It is time to pause to determine how you define yourself before God the Father: As a "child of the world," planted on earth with the sole purpose of being born, growing, reproducing, and dying; and, in the process, worshiping himself and false gods. Or, as a Son of the Highest God, filled with the powerful Holy Spirit that connects him not only with the Father but with his design, purpose, and destiny. It is time to look and inquire into your innermost being, making an honest determination if you have hidden because of ties to the world and do not recognize the need for Christ Jesus to be your Lord and Savior. The Word says: "You shall love the Lord your God with all your heart, and with all your mind, and with all your strength." Deuteronomy 6:5.

The Marriage God Designed

As we have already seen, God created men and women so that they would not be alone but would procreate and have children.

The Father wanted Adam and Eve to share life and nurture their children. Thus, he designed the family system as a means for men and women to fill the earth and exercise dominion over all things, while the Father covers it with His presence. God desires for a male and a female to come together to form a family and have children. God intends for children to grow within a healthy family structure, loving God, being educated in biblical principles, and to love and fear the Lord. The Father, and any decent human being, expects that during the process of growth and maturity, each member of the family structure be allowed to develop their unique and singular virtues; nurture their biological identity, as well as their hearts and minds. Within the family, each member should develop healthy habits that promote relationships and affirm covenants – First with God and second, with each other. There must be a covenant between husband and wife, between parents and children, and a reciprocal covenant between children and parents. The covenant allows for blessings to be manifest.

However, in this era, marriage according to God's original design is no longer honored. This phenomenon is attributed to a lack of knowledge. The fundamental concepts and pillars of marriage and family in today's society have been completely distorted. When man disobeyed God (represented in Adam and Eve), all men turned away from God's grace, rebelled, and were left needing redemption. It is due to rebelliousness that the biblical principles established by God have been modified, allowing society to accept the erosion of biblical truths. Thus, the anthropological reality that men and women complement and need each other for reproduction is denied. Children need a mother and a father to flourish fully. Values about marriage are considered old-fashioned and to modernize the notion of family and marriage, the new and modern society proposes to disconnect from God.

Society turned its beliefs to modify the principles that protect the family. People think that marriage is nothing more than a union sustained by an intense emotion between two or more adults who conceive and consent to it, regardless of whether the encounter is sexual, platonic, exclusive, open, temporary, or permanent. Logically, arrangements such as these leave marriage and family without common form, protection, or purpose, and the children that result from these types of passing encounters are abandoned burdens that the government must support and raise. Children grow up without hope or a healthy future because, from birth, the benefit of parenthood, the security, and the stability that a healthy and functional family can provide is denied.

The real debate lies on a deeper level, as we live in an era of unprecedented cultural confusion. Families are in decline. Children are abused, women and men experience domestic violence in epidemic proportions, couples marry, couples divorce, remarry, form ties, divide, husbands and wives are unfaithful while carrying vast amounts of personal baggage. Today, we have broken families, dysfunctional families, and blended families. The traditional nuclear family, the one in which the father works while the mother cares for the children, is today a family structure that is rapidly losing shape and form. In society, we try to pick up the pieces and create views without God, hoping for a better life, mistakenly believing that it is the way to achieve greater success. No wonder the pieces don't fit, and families perish!

The pair of humans God made is different from all other pairs of animals Adam named. This is because of the particular way in which God formed Eve, also very different from the way God created Adam, although God declared them one flesh. Intentionally and implicitly, the design included the premise that, if neither one separated from God or each other, they would be all right. Men were created to belong, not to be alone. The family needs to live in an integrated way within marriage if they desire to live according to

God's will. God determined His blessing and design for men and women. God also established a healthy social structure from which the fruit of those relationships could be protected, grow, and be productive in society. Within a Godly family system, each child is rewarded with a sense of belonging, a place to develop and flourish, unconditional love, a set of parents – a man and a woman to guide them until physical, emotional, intellectual, and spiritual maturity is achieved and the person becomes of age. In that family nest, each person is created and positioned to develop their unique virtues.

The model is so perfect that even the mother's and father's biological chemistry allows each individual to nurture and develop their sexual identity, free of confusion and with healthy attachments. Every member within this structure develops, is forgiven many times, and is treated with love and compassion. Parents have the responsibility and the opportunity to participate in their children's comprehensive education directly.

In an environment like this, children can start and complete each stage of development, growing healthily and successfully into the next step. Individuals who belong to a healthy family system can grow together, endure life's trials and tribulations, remain together, mature, get married (if they choose to), and form a family. This ideal scenario occurs not only in covenant with God, your partner, and yourself, but also within the family context, where each member can be emotionally, financially, and socially rewarded, both in the short and long term.

Unfortunately, we live amid a world of orphans, because of the lack of fatherhood, men and women walk through life without identity, emotionally wounded, rejected, broken, and with a sense of loss and abandonment. Although we are powerful enough to overcome the challenges that daily life presents, we walk through life unable to recognize who we are, what we possess, or what we represent, and why we are on earth.

Abraham Maslow, a leading American psychologist of the twentieth century, developed the Hierarchy of Needs and represented it with a five-stage pyramid. In the pyramid, Maslow described the order in which humans present their needs and the motivation to fulfill them. These basic human needs must be adequately and timely met for an individual to grow physically, emotionally, mentally, spiritually, and socially in a healthy manner.

In the first stage, for example, a baby needs its physiological needs, such as feeding, sleeping, breathing, and identifying with its protectors, to be provided on time. In this way, the baby will experience healthy development and progress to the next stage. When parents do not take care of their child as required, the baby will progress to the next stage because months and years accumulate, and individuals transition from being babies to children, to adolescents, to adults, and eventually to elders as time marks their seasons. However, they do it with marked deficiencies, to a greater or lesser degree, depending on the amount of care provided or deprived. This beautiful and necessary human being will struggle to develop their identity, and it will be challenging for them to believe that what they do is valuable and has a purpose. It will be challenging for this person to complete the totality of the design God outlined for them, unless they surrender to Jesus Christ and make Him their Lord and Savior. If the individual chooses to make Jesus Lord of their life, this will bring about a Divine Intervention of inner healing and restoration, as I have witnessed many times among God's children, me included, that will change a life forever.

Erik Erikson, a German American psychoanalyst, developed an eight-stage theory of identity and psychosocial development, which explores three aspects of personality. 1) The ego identity (self), 2) personal identity (the idiosyncrasies that distinguish a person from another, and 3) the social and cultural identity (the collection of social roles a person might play). Erikson's psychosocial theory of development examines the impact that external factors, such as parents and society, have on personality development from childhood to adulthood. According to Erikson's theory, every person must pass through a series of eight interrelated stages over the entire life cycle. It also explains what must happen during each stage for the individual to develop into a healthy and productive person.

Stage 1. INFANCY: BIRTH-18 MONTHS OLD

Basic Trust vs. Mistrust – Hope

The child will develop optimism, trust, confidence, and security if adequately cared for. If a child does not experience trust or faith, they may develop insecurity, feelings of worthlessness, and general mistrust.

Stage 2. TODDLER/EARLY CHILDHOOD YEARS: 18 MONTHS TO 3 YEARS

Autonomy vs. Shame – Will

During stage 2, the child can build self-esteem and autonomy as they learn new skills and distinguish right from wrong. The well-cared-for child is sure of himself and behaves with pride rather than shame. It is also the time of the "terrible twos' where defiance, temper tantrums, and stubbornness can also appear. Children tend to be vulnerable during this stage, sometimes feeling shame and low self-esteem due to any inability to learn individual skills, too much prohibition, lack of stimulus, or a handicap.

3. PRESCHOOLER: 3 TO 5 YEARS

Initiative vs. Guilt – Purpose

During the third stage, the child develops a desire to imitate the adults they are close to and attempts to recreate play situations that replicate experiences of being a mother or a father at home. Playing out roles in a trial universe, recreating the blueprint for what he believes an adult role is. This is also the stage during which the individual initiates the struggle of "social role identification." If frustrated over natural desires and goals, he may experience guilt.

Stage 4. SCHOOL-AGE CHILD: 6 TO 12 YEARS

Industry vs. Inferiority – Competence

During this stage, the individual can learn, create, and acquire new skills, thereby developing a sense of industry. Since this is a very social stage of development, if the child experiences unresolved feelings of inadequacy and inferiority among peers, severe problems in terms of competence and self-esteem can develop. During this stage, the most significant relationships are with the school and with peers. Parents are no longer the only authority, although they remain significant to the child.

Stage 5. ADOLESCENT: 12 TO 18 YEARS

Identity vs. Role Confusion – Fidelity

Until this season of a child's life, development depends on what is done to a person. However, from this point forward, development depends primarily upon what a person does. Adolescents must struggle to discover their own identity while navigating social interactions and striving to "fit in." The sense of morality and right from wrong is developed. Some adolescents attempt to delay entrance to adulthood by withdrawing from responsibilities (moratorium).

Stage 6. YOUNG ADULT: 18 TO 35

Intimacy and Solidarity vs. Isolation – Love

During this stage, young adults tend to seek friendships and love or even consider "settling down" to start families. This group seeks deep intimacy and satisfying relationships, but if these are unsuccessful, isolation may result.

Stage 7. MIDDLE-AGED ADULT: 35 TO 55 OR 65

Generativity vs. Self-absorption or Stagnation – Care

Family, career, and work are the most important things at this stage. For this stage, the individual may attempt to produce something that makes a difference to society and fears becoming inactive and meaningless. Thus, some individuals may struggle to find purpose.

8. LATE ADULT: 55 OR 65 TO DEATH

Integrity vs. Despair – Wisdom

The last stage involves much reflection as older adults can look back with a feeling of integrity, contentment, and fulfillment, having led a meaningful life and made a valuable contribution to society. Others may experience a sense of despair during this stage, reflecting on their past experiences and failures. They may fear death and wonder, "What was the point of life? Was it worth it?"

In his book *Homecoming: Reclaiming and Healing Your Inner Child*, John Bradshaw puts it this way:

- **Hope** results when a <u>newborn</u> feels a greater sense of <u>confidence than distrust</u> from his protectors.

- The **Will** results when, <u>in his early years,</u> in his struggle to separate and be born psychologically, a child obtains a greater sense of <u>autonomy or emancipation</u> than <u>shame and doubt</u>.

- The **Purpose** results <u>from the school years,</u> a child develops a <u>greater understanding of</u> industry and creativity than of <u>inferiority</u>.

From these premises, we can appreciate the value and importance of the first years of human existence. The early years are as important as love, healthy attachments, and timely and dedicated care, which will help a little person become a healthy and productive adult, empowered to deliver to humanity all the potential the Father put within them.

Once we surrender our lives to Jesus Christ, the Father begins to reveal why he put us on earth. The only condition is that we must seek His heart to discover our design and purpose. Blessings are obtained because of our intimate relationship and continuous communion with Him.

Let us appreciate how I emphasized that we must approach God, seeking the things we do not know or understand. The reason for this emphasis is that we need to learn them. We must know the heart of the Father. The Bible teaches that "My people perish for lack of knowledge" Hosea 4:6. The vital matter is to remain teachable. Ask Him what He wants to say to you today, and obey!

Jeremiah 33:3

"Call unto me, and I will answer thee, and show thee great and mighty things that you knowest not."

## *The Design Intervened in My Life*

In the first part of my testimony, as outlined in the previous chapters, I described my experiences as a young girl and an adult. I described my life with my parents and their divorce. I explained how this event affected all my siblings and me. I narrated about how I transitioned in life from a very young age and how my family dealt with the struggles and challenges from an early age. Finally, I discussed my marriage and subsequent divorce.

I take full responsibility for my decisions as a young adult. I confess that out of total ignorance about spiritual matters, I chose to live without God, even though several people repeatedly spoke to me about Him and His calling. I understand that I was wrong for not accepting Him, as I missed out on many blessings and the knowledge of His will. I mistakenly used my free will to refuse the gospel of good news because, like most people, I was clinging to the world and what it offers, even though it often brings nothing but sorrow and pain, leaving deep marks and hurts on the heart. Like many people, I settled for what life provides, despite the pain, sadness, and unpleasantness it brings.

Mistakenly, I thought that walking with Christ would be equal to submitting to a religious and boring life, filled with lack and mockery. I also believed that to accept Jesus as my savior, I needed preparation, a cleansing of my soul, and to be free from sin – a condition I did not know how to obtain. I now understand all these ideas are nothing but lies of the devil because Jesus receives us as we are, full of sin and evil-doing, and then helps us in the transformation process for the changes I needed to make. The fact is that Jesus accepts us as we are because He is the one with the power to change us. Jesus heals, transforms our hearts, and frees our minds. If man could change without God, he would. Quoting the Word of

God in the book of Mark 2:17, which says: "The healthy do not need a doctor, but the sick. I have not come to call the righteous but the sinners."

One of the reasons I ended up divorcing my husband was that we did not have God in our lives. If the Lord had been at the center of our lives, we would have worked our troubles out. I mentioned earlier that if I had been more sensitive to His call when I experienced sadness and loneliness, if I had responded to His call, I would not have separated and finally divorced from my first husband. Given the opportunity, our Heavenly Father would have restored our marriage and saved our family from the pain of divorce, as destroying a family is never the best option. When this happens, everyone loses, including the children, or rather, especially the children. However, after twenty years of marriage, we both felt that the wounds each of us carried were irreparable and that there was no other solution to our problems and differences.

At the time, neither one of us understood anything about the Supernatural God who heals. We did not know God takes our misfortunes, often caused by our own decisions to live independently, and turns them into compelling messages that save, heal, and restore lives. I was not aware that God already knew me and called me by my name. So, without God in my heart, when I turned forty, I divorced my husband and returned to the United States to start a new life, having lived in Colombia. What I did not know was that I would have to experience many other calamities. Although I had left my marriage behind, I packed and carried within me a painful burden of bitterness, loneliness, sadness, abandonment, rejection, low self-esteem, and much more. Very lonely and very sad, I began a new life of work, personal development, and restoration, but again, it was my way.

1 Corinthians 1:26-31



The problem is that we seek to do things our way, act independently from God, and insist on thinking that we are no longer going to make mistakes. The problem with that is, within us, we end up carrying a heavy burden of pain accumulated throughout life, and it does not become lighter with the passing of years but heavier. Thus, by that time, I carried not only the burden of pain caused by my own bad decisions and personal experiences, including a rocky twenty-year marriage, but also those I had acquired from my family of origin.

The burdens had become cumbersome and hard to carry; still, I thought that for me, there could be restoration without God. Now I know that this would not be possible because I was blind, hoping that I would not fail again, even though I was still living in darkness. I did not understand that neither I nor the next person in my life, could have any light to guide the way unless Christ was with us.

There was no light in me because I did not know the light, so I continued in my path, but blindly.

*John 8:12*

*"Then Jesus spoke to them again, saying, "I am the light of the world. He who follows Me shall not walk in darkness, but have the light of life."*

Sometime later, after restarting my new life, I met the man who is now my husband. A Colombian who had also separated from his wife, who had also been abandoned by his father, who dragged the burdens of rejection, abandonment, pain, sadness, anger, and more. Besides, and as if that were not enough, he anesthetized his anguish with alcohol. As you can imagine, this combination translated into a sure disaster, and a few years later, we were both ready for another divorce.

Satan continued reaping havoc in my life and was gaining ground. Without knowing, we had given him the right and the authority to rob, kill, and destroy our lives. As I had mentioned earlier, with our decisions, we either legally give God or the devil, the prince of darkness, the right to intervene. Since there are only two kingdoms, and I rejected the Kingdom of God, by default, I had positioned myself in the realm of darkness where Satan rules. He is known as the prince of this world.

Whether these decisions were made out of ignorance or not, they classified us as children of disobedience and servants of the prince of this world, the ruler of darkness. We did not understand that under that government, there is no light, no peace, and no joy for anyone. There is an abundance of spiritual blindness, darkness, and paths of destruction that lead to great harm and death. Although we breathe and seem alive, there is death and an undesirable destiny that results from those choices.

Our reality was that we both yearned to see different things for our lives and that our new marriage would work so that we could be happy individually and together. The problem was that we proposed to achieve it by doing what we had always done, and that is one of the definitions of a fool. We weren't going to make it! Amid our despair and anguish, we found ourselves needing to make some severe changes, and once again, God, the Father, came to the rescue.

The gospel of Jesus Christ had been presented to my husband six times in his adult life, and he had rejected it each time. On six different occasions, through a childhood friend who serves the Lord, God had called my husband to surrender his life to the Lord. This friend had found him in different places of the world and under different circumstances. They had met "by chance' on airplanes in different continents, in gatherings with mutual friends, and he had always rejected the invitation to salvation. Except for this time, it was different, mainly because my husband, Luis, and I were hitting rock bottom. We were both lost without God and felt hopeless. There, in that condition, God the Father rescued us. This time, united in one accord and recognizing that we needed a Savior, we voluntarily gave our lives to Jesus. From that place of despair and brokenness, God began to restore our lives.

# Chapter 4
# God's Plan Intervened

The Temptation and the Fall of Man

Genesis 3:1-6

*"Now the serpent was more cunning than any beast of the field which the* LORD *God had made. And he said to the woman, "Has God indeed said, 'You shall not eat of every tree of the garden'?"*

*And the woman said to the serpent, "We may eat the fruit of the trees of the garden; but of the fruit of the tree which is in the midst of the garden, God has said, 'You shall not eat it, nor shall you touch it, lest you die.'"*

*Then the serpent said to the woman, "You will not surely die. For God knows that in the day you eat of it, your eyes will be opened, and you will be like God, knowing good and evil."*

*So, when the woman saw that the tree was good for food, that it was pleasant to the eyes, and a tree desirable to make one wise, she took of its fruit and ate. She also gave to her husband with her, and he ate."*

In that same spot, in the middle of the Garden, God planted the Tree of Knowledge of Good and Evil. Although God had placed that tree in the middle of the garden, He did not grant the couple the freedom to eat from it. They were allowed to eat from every other tree, and on this matter, he was very precise. The couple was to rule over and tend to the entire garden; they enjoyed continuous access to God's presence, but they had to obey the only restriction placed upon them.

However, they did not obey the one rule given to them: not to eat from the one tree God had designated, because by doing so, by deciding to do their own will, the Father would remove His protective mantle. Adam and Eve had to decide between listening only to God's Voice and thus honor His goodwill or listening to an external voice and disobey. By choosing not to submit to God's orders, they would have to bear the consequences of death as God had announced. Let us see what this dying meant for them.

Genesis 3:7-9

"Then the eyes of both of them were opened, and they knew that they *were* naked, and they sewed fig leaves together and made themselves coverings. And they heard the sound of the LORD God walking in the garden in the cool of the day, and Adam and his wife hid themselves from the presence of the LORD God among the trees of the garden. Then the LORD God called to Adam and said to him, "Where *are* you?"

God does not lie. If He says it, He will do it, and it was so. Adam and Eve ate from the tree and had to die. The sin of disobedience resulted in spiritual death and, eventually, physical death as well. Spiritual death involved the separation from God, to be banished from Paradise, as God placed an angel at the gate of the Garden of Eden so they would not enter after they were cast out.

Losing all blessings included losing:

- The favor and grace of the Father

- Eternal life in His presence

- The relationship with Him

- Health and peace

- The authority over the creation

- Mastery over creation

- The right to govern over the earth

- (they yielded their headship over to Satan when they disobeyed).

Adam and Eve had to face another consequence: The Devil, who deceived them, convincing Eve they would be like God, took advantage of the situation and took away from them the keys of authority that God had given Adam to rule and have dominion over the earth. For a time, Satan took control over creation and men, bringing much evil and suffering to the world.

Due to this human tragedy, mankind's history was divided into two: Man in Paradise and Man expelled from Paradise. This couple ended up hiding, embarrassed, inclined to sin, independent, and in rebellion. Now, they walked with the original design exchanged for an anti-design Satan falsified. The anti-design robbed them of all the blessings God had in store for all His children, including yours and mine. The couple cast out of Paradise was not good because an expelled person will never walk better than one positioned to belong and have dominion over their given territory. God, the Father, placed them in Paradise with authority and the right to govern; He gave them wealth in abundance, health, beauty, and eternity. He accompanied, guided, and taught them. He supported them with His right hand of justice and planned to lead them in the way they should go, just like He promised in Scripture.

*"Fear thou not; for I am with thee: be not dismayed; for I am thy God: I will strengthen thee; yea, I will help thee; yea, I will uphold thee with the right hand of my righteousness."* Isaiah 41:10 King James Version

*The day you eat of the Tree of Knowledge, you will undoubtedly die.*

After God shared and manifested His Paternity to Adam and Eve, without them having to do anything to earn or deserve His attention, He brought them together. He gave them sexuality to multiply and made it a pleasurable act so they would enjoy each other while doing so. Still, Adam and Eve decided to listen to strange voices. By disobeying, they became recipients of the announced consequence: Death (Spiritual and physical). Perhaps it was not easy for them to understand what dying meant, as death was not a part of the original design for men. Death resulted from their sin.

To die was not only a physical experience, but they would experience it in time. The couple's first death was spiritual, and it entered them into a different realm that they did not know or could understand. This spiritual death involved the separation from the Father, His disapproval, which translated into *Spiritual Death* ("Have you eaten from the tree that I commanded you not to eat?"). The transformation of their status from saints, dwelling in God's Presence, to being banished from the garden and separated from the Father was no small matter – it implied the loss of a highly-priced treasure, not as if it were of little or no importance. Their physical death was not immediate but came with time. This new *lifestyle* brought the torment of physical, emotional, and spiritual sickness, having to bear with pain from the curses God imposed upon the earth, and having to live all the adverse circumstances they would experience as man and woman inhabiting the earth but without God. From that moment on, both Adam and Eve would have to live under the continuous manifestation of their earthly and natural state, which at the same time compromised the human race for all generations to come.

God created Satan as a beautiful cherub, designed to be a worshiper. After he claimed for himself, the adoration intended for God and became prideful, God expelled him from heaven. As a result, he found himself in Eden no longer holy and no longer an angelic and perfect being but a fallen one.

In the garden, Satan approached Eve in the form of a snake because snakes roam grasslands. Although he does not invent anything, he is an expert liar, a deceiver, and knows how to distort God's plan for his children and replace them with anti-designs. We cannot deceive ourselves by ignoring or pretending to ignore the kingdom of darkness that exists. The kingdom of darkness is real, well organized, supernatural, powerful, and eternal. However, never nor in any sense, more remarkable or more powerful than the Kingdom of God; that is the difference.

### Isaiah 14:12-14 "**The Fall of Lucifer**

*"How you are fallen from heaven, O Lucifer, son of the morning! How you are cut down to the ground, You who weakened the nations!*

*For you have said in your heart: 'I will ascend into heaven, I will exalt my throne above God's stars; I will also sit on the mount of the congregation. On the farthest sides of the north; I will ascend above the clouds' heights, I will be like the Most High.'*

Contrary to what the devil asserted, the first man and woman died of sadness, shame, pain, and fear. Living without the Father who cared for them with love, their eyes opened to a life that was only physical and not spiritual. Adam and Eve began to experience the difference between living for good and dying for evil. What Satan (dressed as a serpent) said to Eve was a half-truth, that is, a great lie. Instead of "being like God, knowing good and evil," because of their thirst for power and sense of independence, they lost their relationship with God and plunged, not into good but into evil.

In turn, the devil had also developed a plan that consisted of destroying everything God does. He accomplished this task through an anti-design, which is contrary to God's original design. The anti-design starts by breaking our relationship with the Creator. The worship intended for the Heavenly Father is offered to him: the fallen, proud angel and son of perdition. What Lucifer longs for is to be worshiped, and we do this when we disobey God. To this day, Satan exerts influence on men, presenting them with a counterfeit alternative to every perfect gift God has in store for the children of his creation. The problem is that since many do not believe Satan exists, they quickly fall for his tricks, just as he expects.

If we choose to partake of evil, we give way to the spirits of darkness: the devil and his principalities, powers, and rulers of darkness – come to rob, kill, and destroy. Steal the Father's blessings that represent peace and justice, the meaning of abundant life, prosperity, family unity, and all the good God has prepared for every person alive. At all costs, the devil wants to kill our illusions and leave us without a sense of purpose in life. For this reason, the devil leads us to do things that are detrimental to our well-being and those around us. The devil's best and most potent weapon: to make us think that he does not exist!

Ephesians 6:12

*"For we do not wrestle against flesh and blood, but against principalities, against powers, against the rulers of the darkness of this age, against spiritual hosts of wickedness in the heavenly places."*

God's Word teaches us that our struggle is not against other human beings: husbands, sons, brothers, parents, or friends. Instead, our fight is spiritual against spiritual principalities, powers, and rulers that move in our midst. We are spiritual beings, for better or for worse. The battle is against our fallen nature that operates within us. It has to do with the enemy encouraging people from all walks of life towards evil doing because of the devil's plan. Unless, of course, in the exercise of Free Will, man chooses not to be partakers of evil but good and act according to what the Spirit of God guides us to do. All of which is written in His Word and not according to our own opinion.

Genesis 5:3

*"And Adam lived one hundred and thirty years, and begot a son in his likeness, after his image, and named him Seth."*

The Enigma of the Created Man

The Father created, breathed life, and imparted His very nature to man. He was made a holy man (innocent of all evil), just (perfect, righteous), and given free will. We know that when man disobeyed, sin entered him, natural and spiritual death overcame him, and he was cast out from Paradise. The Father ordered them to work the land, live naturally, not supernaturally, bear fruit, subdue the earth, and multiply.

Under this new direction and with no other alternative, they restarted their lives and had two children, Cain and Abel. It is unknown if they were born inside or outside the garden. As time passed, they had Seth, their third son, born in Adam's likeness - with a sinful nature. From this act, all humanity would walk the earth with a nature different from the Heavenly Father's Original Design - His holy image.

It is crucial to note that God's image is still present in all people, but in a broad sense. We maintain the intellectual and creative capacity, the natural faculty for affection, a conscience, and a moral law written in our hearts, which gives conviction over good and evil. We can decide what separates us from the rest of creation (animals). What needs restoration is our likeness to the Father, because we have lost it. Despite this act of love and mercy, there were adverse changes in our image and likeness

caused by the fall of mankind:

- Man's nature corrupted from its seed.
- Holiness and righteousness are no longer naturally present.
- His essence for unconditional love toward all men, not present.

However, whoever "believes in him who justifies the wicked, his faith is counted for righteousness," Romans 4:5. The Father did not leave us without hope, although man needs to repent of his sins and ask for forgiveness to be redeemed. Why? Ephesians 4:22-24 encourages believers to "put off your old self" and "put on the new self," which is created in God's likeness. This involves shedding the former way of life characterized by deceitful desires and being renewed in the spirit of one's mind. It's a call to embrace a transformed identity rooted in righteousness and holiness actively.

We can only achieve changes after we recognize that we need our Creator and voluntarily return to seek him. Achieving change means leaving the old man behind, to recover the image of the One who created us; until obtaining full knowledge, where Christ is everything in all things.

We can conclude that the cause of our sinful nature is not exclusively attributable to losing the image of God. After being expelled from the garden, humanity's contaminated, seared conscience is what led to their sinful actions and attitudes. Man lost their spiritual nature and communion with the Heavenly Father and fell into a continuous decline. No wonder it is known as "the fall." After being removed from the Glory of God, he became a soulish being (natural, emotional, willful), who, when reproducing himself, does so according to the Adamic image he inherited and knows.

## Man in need of God

In the same way that the Spirit of God surrounds us and lives within those who invite him and give him the legal right to remain in them, so does Satan and his spiritual hosts. He surrounds and inhabits those who give him the legal right to stay within them. This indwelling is a 'possession.' A man can be possessed even if he or she opts not to believe it. I mentioned that the devil's greatest warfare weapon is to make men think he does not exist. Ignoring Satan does not mean that he does not walk freely, at ease, executing his plans with the mere objective of robbing men of God's Design and replacing it with his destructive anti-design. Of course, neither God nor the devil can inhabit our body nor possess it without being invited. Either one can influence us to accept their presence. The invitation is not always extended merely with words. The invitation is also conveyed through facts, behaviors, actions, and sin. For example, an alcoholic invites the demon, or spirit of alcoholism, to dwell in him through continuous drunkenness. One who watches pornography invites the spirit of sexual immorality to inhabit him, leading to a state of moral decline hard to break and capable of destroying any normalcy in his life. Similarly, one who seeks communion with the Father invites the Holy Spirit to abide in them, destroy the devil's works, and set them free.

Fallen nature has caused humanity's spiritual faculties to be severely compromised, and their original supernatural nature to be silenced. With the spirit in them silenced, mankind developed a physical, emotional, and intellectual capacity that neglects the God-given spiritual gifts, which have become dormant. Man ceased to be the spiritual being who lives in the supernatural realm and became a natural being, where what he knows (intellect), what he feels (emotions), and what he wants to do (will) predominate. He lives unequivocally, believing that his value lies in what he does and owns, not in who he is in Christ Jesus. Devoid of identity and very concerned about doing whatever it takes to impress. When men abandon the principles that God establishes to protect them from falling into the enemy's clutches, they begin to experience situations or circumstances that lead to failure, anguish, and insecurity. He starts to roll in evil-doing until he immerses himself in Toxic Shame, where the enemy wants to drag all humanity with no exceptions. Satan intends to place us in positions where we cannot get out without generating all kinds of losses, such as broken relationships, destroyed marriages, divorces, abortions, loss of trust and credibility, persecution, and financial failures, among many others.

*Acts 13:10*

*"¡and said, "O full of all deceit and all fraud, you son of the devil, you enemy of all righteousness, will you not cease perverting the straight ways of the Lord?"*

I invite you to read the following descriptive and revealing poem, "My Name is Toxic Shame," written by Reverend Leo Booth, Minister Theologian, and Dr. John Bradshaw. PhD, Author, Theologian, and Family Counselor. In this poem, the authors describe how Satan destroys while men, as if asleep, entertain themselves with life, thinking that he does not exist.

**"My Name Is Toxic Shame" -Rev. Leo Booth & Dr. John Bradshaw**

I was there at your conception.

In the epinephrine of your mother's shame

You felt me in the fluid of your mother's womb

I came upon you before you could speak

Before you understood

Before you had any way of knowing

I came upon you when you were learning to walk

When you were unprotected and exposed

When you were vulnerable and needy

Before you had any boundaries

My name is Toxic Shame

I came upon you when you were magical

Before you could know I was there

I severed your soul

I pierced you to the core

I brought you feelings of being flawed and defective

I brought you feelings of distrust, ugliness, stupidity,

doubt, worthlessness, inferiority, and unworthiness

I made you feel different

I told you there was something wrong with you

I soiled your Godlikeness

My name is Toxic Shame

I existed before the conscience

Before guilt, before morality

I am the master emotion

I am the internal voice that whispers words of condemnation

I am the internal shudder that courses through you without any
mental preparation

My name is Toxic Shame

I live in Secrecy.

In the deep moist banks of darkness, depression, and despair

Always I sneak up on you

I catch you off guard

I come through the back door

Uninvited, unwanted

The first to arrive

I was there at the beginning of time With Father Adam, Mother Eve,
Brother Cain

I was at the Tower of Babel, the Slaughter of the Innocents

My name is Toxic Shame

I come from "shameless" caretakers, abandonment, ridicule,

abuse, neglect, perfectionist systems

I am empowered by the shocking intensity of a parent's rage

The cruel remarks of siblings

The jeering humiliation of other children

The awkward reflection in the mirrors

The touch that feels icky and frightening

The slap, the pinch, the jerk that ruptures trust

I am intensified by a racist, sexist culture

The righteous condemnation of religious bigots

The fears and pressures of schooling

The hypocrisy of politicians

The multigenerational shame of dysfunctional family systems

My name is Toxic Shame

I can transform a woman person, a gay person, and an Oriental
person, a precious child into

A bitch, a bull dyke, a faggot, a chink, a selfish little bastard

I bring chronic pain

A pain that will not go away

I am the hunter that stalks you night and day

Every day, everywhere

I have no boundaries

You try to hide from me but you cannot

Because I live inside of you

I make you feel hopeless

Like there is no way out

My name is Toxic Shame

My pain is so unbearable that you must pass me on to others

Through control, perfectionism, contempt, criticism, blame,

envy, judgment, power, and rage

My pain is so intense

You must cover me up with addictions, rigid roles,

reenactment, and unconscious ego defenses

My pain is so intense that you must numb out and no longer feel me

I convinced you that I am gone – that I do not exist

You experience absence and emptiness.

My name is Toxic Shame

I am the core of co-dependency

I am spiritual bankruptcy

The logic of absurdity

The repetition of compulsion

I am crime, violence, incest, rape

I am the voracious hole that fuels all addictions

I am instability and lust

I twist who you are into what you do and have murdered your soul.

And you pass me on for generations.

My name is Toxic Shame.

Now we understand how and why disobedience and rebellion have had such devastating spiritual and natural effects on all of humanity, leaving it in spiritual bankruptcy and requiring punishment first and redemption afterwards. In this chapter, we learn what God's Punishment means, and in the fifth chapter, we discover how, through Jesus Christ, He saves us.

This spiritual bankruptcy brought many ramifications and consequences that still, to this day, perverts humanity's soul. After undergoing the radical change that came over Adam and Eve, their lives became difficult. Man is not a physical being (of flesh and bones) on a spiritual journey; on the contrary, man is a spiritual being on a physical and, more importantly, a temporary journey.

Romans 5:17-18

*"For if by the one man's [a]offense death reigned through the one, much more those who receive abundance of grace and the gift of righteousness will reign in life through the One, Jesus Christ.) Therefore, as through [b]one man's offense judgment came to all men, resulting in condemnation, even so through one[c] Man's righteous act the free gift came to all men, resulting in justification of life."*

There is so much pain in humanity, and society continues to sink deeper into moral decay every day. All this because:

1. In Adam and Eve, all men have sinned, been made aware of their nakedness, lost their innocence, and are filled with shame - a consuming poison. The nakedness of the soul and spirit is nothing other than being without identity, empty, and without God's presence.

2. In Adam and Eve, all men listened to the majestic Voice of God with embarrassment and fear; therefore, they decided to hide and not listen to it - they moved away from the only one who could help them. An action that generated the sense of independence prevented them from knowing God's will; therefore, each one acts as they see fit.

3. When God called them, they did not face their act of disobedience; instead, they blamed each other and projected their responsibility, which prevented them from repenting. It will never be easy for a man to recognize that he and not someone else needs to repent of sin, and his need to make changes, generating the Toxic Shame that invades him and from which he needs to free himself.

4. In Adam and Eve, man lost the Image and Likeness of God and acquired Adam's nature, sinful and weak, while the Spirit of God was silenced and needed revival.

Psalm 51:17

"The sacrifices of God *are* a broken spirit,

A broken and a contrite heart—

These, O God, You will not despise."

The fear that the male and female felt was in no way the Holy Fear of God, which is reverent and generated not by fear, but by love and the desire not to hurt the heart of the Father who loves man so much love and to whom we profess fidelity. That fear is very different from what they felt.

## The Redeemed Man Changes

God's limits on Adam and Eve in the Garden of Eden were not just a whim. The purpose of the boundary was to develop an excellent use of their free will, teach them the value of subjection to authority, and develop the character necessary to comply with the assignment given - is it not the same thing that we propose for our children?

Everything God designed for the first couple was motivated by his love and mercy towards them. His plan was also to extend his goodness to future generations because it would fulfill his perfect dream. Think about this for a moment. Isn't that the same thing that we as parents propose for our children? The limits that we must maintain in our lives are nothing more than fences of protection. Boundaries act like hedges that place us in positions to decide between doing what is right and what is not profitable. Obeying God's Word is necessary for us and others. God does not want us to walk in lawlessness and disorder on earth. However, our actions indicate that we like to push limits until we are completely removed, leaving us unprotected, feeling insecure, and totally at the mercy of the evil that continually haunts our lives.

A redeemed person changes when they are serious about their inner healing and the detoxification of their soul. He understands inner healing will help him get closer to God, hear his voice, purify his soul, and restore relationships, including the one with himself. Inner healing is a process achieved through a series of small and consistent changes that will yield a transformation by renewing the mind. Changes in the way of thinking help change actions, and changes in attitudes change the course of being. The repentant man is persuaded that Jesus is "the Way, the Truth, and the Life," therefore, he begins to act according to the plan of God established in His Word. However, when the responsibility is placed on someone else, one can determine whether a change is not required, because, after all, they are not guilty. By nature, man resists change because it is a process that hurts and requires a condition free of pride and rigidity, but with a sensitive and teachable heart, which is not easy to achieve. God's Word defines this condition as a contrite and humbled heart that God does not despise.

But God demonstrates his love for us in this: While we were still sinners, Christ died for us. "So, by the transgression of one came condemnation to men, just as by the righteousness of one came the justification of life to all men." Romans 5:8, 18. It is through Christ Jesus, our Redeemer, that the Father restores is image in us. We can voluntarily decide to accept Him as our Savior and renounce our sinful nature to fulfill His purpose with the free will granted to us. We do this with faith, and "Faith is counted for righteousness." Romans 4:5.

## *My second opportunity*

A few years after my second marriage, our relationship became difficult, complicated, and strained. We did not have the same ideals or goals in life, and our burdens were cumbersome. He was also divorced and did not know God. Although the conflicts between us were caused by reasons different from those in my first marriage, the second one became almost as complicated and problematic as the first. Before our fifth anniversary, we were already considering divorce, and in fact, we had already separated.

For the second time in our lives, we felt like there was no way out. We tried with all our abilities to do everything the world says it takes to be a successful person and make our relationship work, but we sank deeper and deeper into despair. We both carried the type of emotional burdens that did not facilitate change, although we knew we needed to change radically. We both lived by the models we had of failed families, and nothing went right for us. We were about to impose a second divorce upon ourselves and once again lose everything we believed. In that place, plunged in the pit of despair, our salvation came when one day, someone merciful preached the Word of God to us. By His Grace and mercy, Christ presented Himself to save and restore us and, with his power and authority, took charge to change our future. At that point, we were desperate and hit rock bottom.

To invite Jesus means to give Him the legal right to take charge. With the heart, we give him access to our lives to change and heal all the things that hinder the operation of His perfect will and destroy God's design.

We were determined to allow Jesus Christ to be Lord of our lives and the restorer of our marriage, and to guide all our decisions. Immediately after surrendering our lives, our walk with Christ began, and we see his work perfected in us. After knowing the Lord and His plans, we decided to seek His blessings in our marriage and had a Christian wedding celebration, just as He commands.

Today, I can say that Jesus is our light and our salvation (Psalms 27:1). Light because we walked in darkness when we were lost; now He is the light that guides our way. 2) Salvation because Jesus delivered us from (spiritual) death, and we were born to a new life, eternal and lasting, both here on earth and in heaven. In a new book, on a new page, the book of life, He wrote our names. He tore the book we were writing on and never recalled it. Jesus says in Ezekiel 16:9-10: "Then I washed you with water; yes, I thoroughly washed off your blood, and I anointed you with oil. I clothed you in embroidered cloth and gave you the fine linen and covered you with silk." This verse exemplifies how the Holy Spirit takes away our pain, washes away our wounds, and covers us with His love and justice. He dressed us in fine and resplendent linen - His Holiness. By his grace, Jesus forgave us, and with his passion, freed us from (spiritual) death.

My husband and I gave our lives to him when our world was darkening, and we had nowhere to go. Today, twenty years later, we offer all glory to Jesus Christ and our sincere gratitude for transforming our weeping into dancing and clothing us with joy. We honor Him because of His faithfulness to fulfill His promise to make each of us new creatures. We desperately needed a change, and Jesus, as Lord and Savior, rescued us.

He covers us with mercy and goodness when we completely trust him and recognize, without hesitation, that he is our refuge, our fortress, our Protector. He delivers without failing or fainting on all his promises. When we fully believe and put our faith and hope in the Lord, no matter what is happening around us, whether it is anxiety, fear, worry, doubt, or divorce, everything dissipates because God is greater than any adverse circumstance. When the

Lord cares for us, we are truly protected. Jesus took away our pain and restored our marriage. He will also do it for you. If you ask him and allow him to heal your illness, your relationships with your spouse, children, parents, or friends, your heart or emotions, He will step in to do miracles and help you fulfill your Divine Purpose.

Philippians 4:6-8

*"Be anxious for nothing, but in everything by prayer and supplication, with thanksgiving, let your request be made known to God; and the peace of God, which surpasses all understanding, will guard your hearts and minds through Christ Jesus. Finally, brethren, whatever things are true, whatever things are noble, whatever things are just, whatever things are pure, whatever things are lovely, whatever things are of good report, if there is any virtue and if there is anything praiseworthy – meditate on these things.*

I know that there are different dysfunctions in families and that no one can claim that everything is or was perfect in their home. As in many other families, in my family of origin, we experienced a certain level of dysfunction. My siblings and I were exposed to a tremendous amount of pain, despair, confusion, and sadness, which manifested in the form of anger, depression, aggressiveness, impatience, independence, denying God, and developing a tremendous ability to seek achievements.

A Spanish "quote" says there is a little musician, a poet, and "some craziness" inside each one of us. I believe that the musical and poetic aspects are God-given gifts, and that the craziness represents the legacy we receive from our families of origin and our journey through life. Of course, the level of anger we all experience will depend on the nature of the family dysfunctions. Furthermore, most of our follies or confusions allow us to function civilly and be part of a society in which these shortcomings can be assimilated rather well. This craziness occurs because we are, to no small extent, the product of our experiences, especially those of our early years, within our families of origin. Those experiences from childhood mark us forever, and although it is possible to heal those wounds, they must be acknowledged, surrendered, and worked through. What is not true is that time erases everything. I experienced firsthand that God restores and heals everything when we allow Him to dig deep into our souls. This is my life testimony.

Sometime after my conversion to the Lord, I had a dream which I am going to share because God speaks to us through dreams many times: I was conversing with Abba (Hebrew word that means daddy), and in my hand, there was a pink crystal base, fine, expensive, and beautiful. This crystal was overflowing with oil (oil represents anointing) but broken at the top. The Lord let me know that I represented the crystal base, to which I replied that it was lovely but broken and useless. To my comment, He answered in a sweet and loving tone, "*We are going to repair it.*" Almost all of us come to the feet of Christ, broken and needing to be restored. We cannot see the number of gifts and talents given to us to fulfill our purpose in that condition, much less use them for our good or to influence others positively.

Now I serve him, I recognize Him as my Lord and Savior. I have been free from the oppression and the fruitless search for what is perishable. Without so much struggle, the Lord faithfully prospered us, and we lack nothing in life. Finally, I have come to understand that no matter how much money I have, on the day of my departure for eternity, money and material things will be precisely the first things we leave behind. My Eternal God will not ask me about the money I have accumulated but will want to know about the legacy I left on earth because I completed my assignment - my purpose on earth.

# Chapter 5
## Our Heavenly Father's Redemption Plan

Genesis 3:21

*"Also for Adam and his wife, the LORD God made tunics of skin, and clothed them."*

By His mercy, and amid the relational crisis that broke out between Adam and Eve after they were expelled from the Garden of Eden, God still intervened by bringing them the hope that would mark the restored future of all humanity. He started by dressing them so they would not be ashamed, since the covers they had made for themselves were not enough. The leaves that Adam and Eve made for themselves were nothing more than an attempt to cover up as they saw fit. However, Abba Father manifested his goodwill and love by dressing them in animal skin robes, for which He sacrificed and shed the blood of animals. The shedding of blood signaled the redemption plan for humanity and was in God's heart from the very beginning. It is a shadow and sign of what was to come, except *the blood sacrifice had to be much higher to restore man's relationship with the Father.*

When a man refuses to be ruled by the Creator, he places himself in the position of being his god by doing what he wants. This is why we hear that such a person lives without God or hope. People who opt to live without God often use their God-given talents to seek out pleasures for their delight; they try to solve problems their way, which can create conflicts stemming from their sense of independence and self-sufficiency. They do not discover or fulfill their purpose on earth, much less give God Glory for anything. After all, it was they and not God who created the blessings they enjoy. A life lived independently from the Father results in separation from His will, causing expulsion from the Kingdom of God.

Matthew 10:28

*"And do not fear those who kill the body but cannot kill the soul. But rather fear Him who is able to destroy both soul and body in hell."*

God created all men to depend on and live in total reliance on Him. Those who believe in this written truth will spend eternity with the Heavenly Father, and those who refuse to accept and obey it will spend it in hell. This truth needs to be exposed to the world, as people erroneously believe God has destined everyone to go to heaven when they die, but this is not so. There are conditions to adhere to and knowledge, and one of them is obeying His commands, all of them written in the Scriptures. Men also mistakenly believe the devil and hell do not exist. The Bible tells us that hell is a place of eternal torment and that it is real. Men should not feed on these false concepts because this error can and will cost them an eternity without Jesus Christ. It is absurd to expect an invitation to spend eternity with the Father, the Son, and the Holy Spirit in the House of the Lord when, while on earth, we refused to allow God to enter our hearts or govern our world. Don't you think so?

Mark 9:47-48

*"And if your eye causes you to sin, pluck it out. It is better for you to enter the kingdom of God with one eye, rather than having two eyes, to be cast into hell fire where the worm does not die, and the fire is not quenched."*

Jesus Christ, our Lord, was conceived by the work and Grace of the Holy Spirit, born of the Virgin Mary, to die for men; to redeem men from their sin and to restore the relationship with the Heavenly Father. Jesus' ministry began at the age of thirty and lasted three and a half years, during which He preached and taught the Word, healed the sick, cast out demons, and proclaimed the Kingdom of God. His physical presence on earth divided humanity's history into the "before" and "after" (also known as BC and AD). At the age of thirty-three, he voluntarily took upon himself all of mankind's sins - past, present, and future. The purpose of this enormous sacrifice was to bless humanity with SALVATION.

Jesus' physical death and resurrection on the third day granted eternal life and access to the Father's presence to those who believe in and receive Him as Lord and Savior. The prophets prophesied the life of Jesus on earth as it is written in the Scriptures. Jesus did not die without all the prophecies written about Him coming to pass. This demonstrated that He was not improvising but executing what God the Father had established to bless men through Him.

John 3:16

*"For God so loved the world that He gave His only begotten Son, that whoever believes in Him should not perish but have everlasting life."*

God the Father loves humanity so much that He predetermined that the best He had, His only Son, would suffer and die for all of mankind. God did not send His Son to judge or condemn the world, but to offer men Salvation and Redemption. Although the Son of God never sinned, Jesus became sin so that we would be justified by the power of His Blood Sacrifice. He assumed responsibility and punishment for all of mankind who sinned. The Son of God had to experience brokenness, rejection, oppression, pain, and undergo systematic torture to destroy and uproot him from his natural and spiritual existence. All so we could be perfected through the afflictions He endured in our place.

Jesus had to be rejected and separated from the Creator's Love and protection when the wrath of the Father fell upon him. Whipped thirty-nine times so that by His wounds we would be healed; He became poor so that we would be prosperous and blessed. They stripped Him of all garments until He was half-naked; arms and legs extended to nail Him to the wooden cross. Jesus was nailed to a tree, suffered dehydration and massive blood loss, and experienced circulatory and respiratory obstruction due to the position he was hanged in for many hours. The multiple blows disfigured His face; His temples and forehead lacerated with the crown of thorns placed on His head; they pulled out His beard and put vinegar on His lips when he said he was thirsty, instead of giving Him water. Men mocked Him because He did not come down from the cross after having declared that He was the Son of God. Even his people who professed much love for Him abandoned Him, as it is written. However, Jesus Christ did not complain. He understood that fulfilling the Father's purpose on earth was His reason for existing. Jesus experienced temptation and surrendered His will until He fulfilled His purpose on earth. His painful spiritual death consisted of having to experience separation from His Heavenly Father when He went to the bottomless pit of hell. In the prisons of hell, Jesus declared victory over death and sin, humiliated Satan, and took away the keys of authority Adam had given the deceiver. There on the cross, Jesus irrevocably and eternally defeated the enemy of our lives. Jesus's death and the blood He shed granted men the victory of redemption once and for all. On the cross, Jesus paid in full for all men's sins, diseases, curses, and sicknesses.

Salvation is not by works but by Grace. There is nothing mankind can do to obtain salvation, and no effort could ever be superior to Jesus's sacrifice on the cross. Christ's life fully paid the price for our eternal life. God's Grace is undeserved favor, a gift from the Father because of His love for mankind. Naturally, no one rejects a gift that someone gives them because they understand it is an expression of love and an affirmation of the relationship maintained. Nor do they attempt to pay for the present but receive and appreciate it. However, it is complicated to believe, receive, and finally accept the gift of salvation as undeserved Grace from the Father.

Those who crucified the Messiah, Savior of the world, did not understand that Jesus was not obligated or victimized on the cross. He was born for this moment, and as such, he lived. At the time, death by crucifixion was a sentence for the worst criminals, murderers, and traitors of the Roman Empire. It was the most humiliating way to die. However, Jesus accepted it out of obedience to the Father, knowing an incredible amount of pain awaited him, yet He submitted. Jesus clearly understood the victory His death would bring in favor of all humanity, but also that He was the bridge that would restore man's direct access to our Heavenly Father.

When Jesus died, the thick and heavy curtain separating the Holy Place from the Most Holy Place of the Temple tore from top to bottom. The tearing of the curtain meant the sacrifice presented for the atonement of all men had been sufficient. The Father Himself could eliminate the separation that existed between Himself and humanity. It was God saying, "Men no longer have to remain outside; you can enter into my presence because my Son has restored the way." Additionally, while still on earth, men can benefit from and enjoy His complete work and all the blessings He has given us. Jesus' sacrifice on the cross not only brought the gift of eternity in His presence but also broke every curse on the earth. Any curse or affliction operating in your life, dear reader, be it illness, poverty, addiction, depression, or any other yoke imposed on your life, has already been broken - Christ annulled it. His sacrifice on the cross broke all the chains that bind innate sin in human nature, which is the cause and consequence of mankind's fallen nature without God.

In the book of Romans, Chapter 12:2, Apostle Paul says: "Do not conform to this age, but transform yourself through the renewal of your understanding, so that you may verify what is the good will of God, pleasant and perfect." In other words, he instructs us not to accommodate ourselves to the system of the world but to renew our understanding in light of His Word, which manifests His goodwill and invites us to come closer to know the eternal Father more intimately.

Romans 10:8-10

*"But what does it say? The Word is near you, in your mouth and your heart" (that is, the Word of Faith which we preach): that if you confess with your mouth the Lord Jesus and believe in your heart that God has raised Him from the dead, you will be saved. For with the heart, one believes unto righteousness, and with the mouth, confession is made unto salvation."*

How does Christian Life begin?

The Christian life begins with the confession of Faith. That is, a declaration made with Faith through which one invites Jesus Christ to be the Lord and Savior of our life. The words we profess, the declarations of the mouth, have a lot of power. In the spiritual world, this confession produces a powerful transformation known as "Born again." Whoever makes such a statement remains the same in the natural realm, but it is not so. Whoever confesses Jesus as Lord and Savior is completely transformed. First, the person goes from being an individual, created by God, to being called a 'Son of God' - a significant difference.

John 1:12

*"But as many as received Him, to them He gave the right to become children of God, to those who believe in His name."*

Whether we understand it or not, one cannot take lightly the number of Spiritual Events that take place when a person is born again. I wish someone had taught me these miracles when I was younger, when I did not accept Jesus as my Lord. Due to a lack of knowledge about God's will for my life, I perished for not acknowledging God's invitation.

One of the best-known verses in the Bible is found in the book of Hebrews, chapter 11:1: "Faith, then, is the certainty of what is expected, the conviction of what is not seen." Faith is the certainty of what we cannot see but know to be real and exist. Men's confession or profession of Faith grants entrance to the Kingdom of Light. Through Faith in Christ, man can decide to separate from sin and maintain a life of communion and intimacy with God. Why?

To provide further clarity on this subject, let us revisit the beginning. Before Creation, God the Father existed together with the Son and with the Holy Spirit. It is for this reason that on the sixth day of Creation, when He made man, Genesis 1:26 says, "Let us make man in our image, according to our likeness." Additionally, in Genesis 1:2, Scripture says, "The Spirit of God was moving over the waters," which refers to the Holy Spirit, the Third Person of the Trinity.) Later in the Book of John 1:1:

John 1:1

> *(1)* In the beginning was the Word, and the Word was with God, and the Word was God,
>
> *(2)* He was in the beginning with God.
>
> *(3)* All things were made through Him, and without Him, nothing was made that was made.
>
> *(4)* In Him was life, and the life was the light of men.

The doctrine of the Trinity is one of Christianity's mysteries, believed by Faith. It means that only one God exists as three distinct persons: the Father, the Son, and the Holy Spirit. God's essence is one in three persons, each with a different function, all operating with and for Mankind.

The Scriptures speak of:

• The Father as God in Philippians 1:2: "Grace and peace to you, from God our Father and the Lord Jesus Christ."

• Jesus Christ as God in Titus 2:13: "Waiting for the blessed hope and the glorious manifestation of our great God and Savior Jesus Christ."

• The Holy Spirit as God in Acts 5:3-4, "And Peter said, Ananias, why did Satan fill your heart so that you would lie to the Holy Spirit, and subtract from the price of inheritance? Holding her back, didn't it stay with you? And sold, was it not in your possession? Why did you put this in your heart? You have not lied to men, but God. "

We know God, the Father, is in heaven and gave us his Son, Jesus Christ. He gave us Salvation by Grace and now sits at the right hand of the Father. When Jesus Christ ascended into heaven to sit at the Father's right hand, He also gave us a powerful gift on the day of Pentecost: The Holy Spirit.

The Holy Spirit dwells in the hearts of the children of God on Earth.

John 14:26

*" But the Helper, the Holy Spirit, whom the Father will send in My name, He will teach you all things, and bring to your remembrance all things that I said to you. "*

The Holy Spirit fills all believers and dwells within each man or woman causing them to desire to live in continuous intimacy with the Father, the Son, and the Holy Spirit. God's kingdom flows through to bless others and manifest the Glory of God.

Apostle Guillermo Maldonado, an authority versed in the gospel of Christ, and my Spiritual father for twenty years, has written numerous books about the Kingdom of God, including several bestsellers. In his book, The Kingdom of Power, he quotes the following biblical verses:

• "The Kingdom of God is a kingdom of power and not only of words" (1Corinthians 4:20)

• "It is supernatural" (John 18:36)

• "It is unshakable" (Hebrews 12:28)

• "Repent because the kingdom of heaven has drawn near."

(Matthew 4:17) (G. Maldonado, pg.18-21).

In his book, The Glory of God, he writes: "The Glory of God is the essence of all that God is. When we enter the Glory of God, we inhabit his presence, receive his love and Grace, understand his heart, know his will, and experience his divine power. "

Dr. Myles Monroe, in his book, 'Rediscovering the Kingdom', wrote:

1. "The simple strategy of God to extend and establish His Kingdom on this earth, is to govern this visible world of man from an invisible kingdom of the Spirit.

2. The plan means that man would be His visible representative, explicitly created to live in the natural kingdom to represent it.

3. The original purpose and God intended to rule what is seen, from what is not seen (the Spirit of God in man which is not seen (the spirit of man and the physical body) over the scene on earth. (Monroe, p. 39).

What else can we say about the Kingdom of God? I will extract the answer from the book, *The Glory of God,* authored by Apostle Guillermo Maldonado:

"The Kingdom of God is His sovereign government on earth. It is the realm and foundation of God's power on earth; it is his dominion to establish His will in the lives of His people, here and now, through the redemptive work of His Son, Jesus Christ. God rules over territories, entities, and human beings. He rules over sickness, poverty, and oppression. He is sovereign over the spiritual enemy, Satan, the devil, who seeks to expand his kingdom of darkness in the world, to oppose the Kingdom of the Light of God." (Maldonado p.15, 2013).

On a spiritual level, there are only two known Kingdoms:

• The Kingdom of God – also known as the Kingdom of Light

• The Kingdom of Satan – also known as the kingdom of Darkness

Nowhere in the Bible does it mention an intermediate place where a person can go when they die, not even temporarily. All of mankind live in the realm of the living, called earth, or in eternity, the place where one goes when one dies. When a person's time on earth ends, they go to one of only two eternal places:

1. Heaven with His Creator and Heavenly Father, or

2. Hell with Satan, where the fire burns but does not consume.

When one reaches one of these two places, he or she will remain there for an infinite period, hopelessly and without the possibility of returning. The opportunities for salvation are offered while on earth, but unfortunately not after.

It is essential to give an accurate and valid description of the second and opposite realm in which man can choose to live when his eternity is not with Christ. It is known as the Kingdom of Darkness, already mentioned above. It is the place where men go because they choose to bow before something or someone other than Jesus Christ. Those who are sent to hell chose to worship or offer adoration to a false deity, such as Satan, Asherah, Buddha, saints, materialism, anything or anyone other than Jesus Christ, and refused the invitation to partake of God's Kingdom and perfect will.

The kingdom of darkness is the kingdom where something or someone is considered more important than Jesus. The ruler of the Kingdom of Darkness is Satan, also known as Lucifer, the devil. Although he is already defeated, we must recognize that he has an organized kingdom with a well-established army for the time he has left, and that men fall easily into his deceiving tricks. The Bible says that Satan can manifest himself as an angel of light or a beautiful spiritual entity, although he is not.

Exodus 20: 1-6

*"And God spoke all these words, saying: "I am the* LORD *your God, who brought you out of the land of Egypt, out of the house of* [a]*bondage. You shall have no other gods before Me. You shall not make for yourself a carved image—any likeness of anything that is in heaven above, or that is in the earth beneath, or that is in the water under the earth; you shall not bow down to them nor* [b]*serve them. For I, the* LORD *your God, am a jealous God, visiting*[c] *the iniquity of the fathers upon the children to the third and fourth generations of those who hate Me, but showing mercy to thousands, to those who love Me and keep My commandments.*

As part of my testimony written at the end of each chapter of this book, I shared that I was born in Colombia and grew up in a Catholic family. I clearly understand that Catholics are Christians who believe that Jesus Christ is the Son of God and that Catholicism shares some beliefs with other Christian practices. I am aware that some of the essential Catholic beliefs include that the Bible is inspired by the Holy Spirit, error-free, and the revealed Word of God. Christianity is founded on the values of the Holy Trinity, God the Father, the Son, and the Holy Spirit, as a central principle.

Christianity is an important world belief that stems from the life, teachings, and death of Jesus. Roman Catholicism is the largest of the three major branches of Christianity. Thus, all Roman Catholics are Christians, but not all Christians are Roman Catholic. Nonetheless, it is clear that the same God is preached at the evangelical church and is the essence of this book. As I was writing these pages, I recalled an experience I had soon after my conversion to Christianity, and I want to share it because I consider it relevant and essential to the point I am trying to make.

One day, I was listening to a Catholic radio station and heard the Nicene or Apostolic Creed. I had repeated it many times in the masses I attended since I was a little girl, to the extent that I knew it by heart. However, that day, each word had a profound impact on my heart and in my spirit, and as I listened and repeated the Nicene Creed, I understood the meaning of each phrase. I was amazed that I had mechanically repeated it so many times but had never discerned the meaning of each word of the creed until that moment. It emphasizes Jesus came down from heaven "for our salvation" and by the work of the Holy Spirit, was incarnated in Mary, the Virgin, and became man; and for our cause was crucified in the time of Pontius Pilate; he suffered and was buried and rose again on the third day, according to the Scriptures, and he ascended into heaven and is sitting at the right hand of the Father. "

The Creed is indeed a profession of Faith prayed at the end of each Mass. In the same way, professed Christians who believe with all their hearts that Jesus is Lord declare, with revelation and a profound sense of repentance for their sins, that they voluntarily make a covenant with Jesus for all eternity. And they are saved. This profession of faith grants men and women two things. First, the right to be called children of God the Father and eternal life with Him. This is possible by the sacrifice of Jesus Christ on the cross. This is what the blood sacrifice of Jesus bought for all humanity: salvation and eternal life. This is not revealed to men by blood and flesh but the Spirit of God who comes to dwell in them, as the best gift for all men who accept.

However, it is surprising to me when, from an Evangelical (biblical) position, I speak to people about this same Christ and this same sacrificial work, and they reject the message because they maintain that: "they are not going to change their religion."


Let's read: The Nicene or Apostolic Creed.


"Nicene Creed:

We believe in one God,
the Father, the Almighty
maker of heaven and earth,
of all that is, seen and unseen.
We believe in one Lord, Jesus Christ,
the only Son of God,
eternally begotten of the Father,
God from God, Light from Light,
true God from true God,
begotten, not made,
of one Being with the Father.
Through him all things were made.
For us men and for our salvation
he came down from heaven:
by the power of the Holy Spirit
he became incarnate from the Virgin Mary, and was made man.
For our sake he was crucified under Pontius Pilate;
he suffered death and was buried.
On the third day he rose again
in accordance with the Scriptures;

he ascended into heaven
and is seated at the right hand of the Father.
He will come again in glory to judge the living and the dead,
and his kingdom will have no end. We believe in the Holy Spirit,
the Lord, the giver of life,
who proceeds from the Father and the Son.
With the Father and the Son, he is worshipped and glorified.
He has spoken through the Prophets. We believe in one holy,
catholic, and apostolic church.
We acknowledge one baptism for the forgiveness of sins.
We look for the resurrection of the dead,
and the life of the world to come. Amen".

Romans 10:8-10

*"And if Christ is in you, the body is dead because of sin, but the Spirit is life because of righteousness. But if the Spirit of Him who raised Jesus from the dead dwells in you, He who raised Christ from the dead will also give life to your mortal bodies through His Spirit who dwells in you."*

The late Evangelist Billy Graham wrote: "Heaven will be a glorious place of life that will have no end. Unimaginable joy, eternal peace, pure love, indescribable beauty - it is what we will see in heaven. But more significant than all, we will see the presence of God the Father, God the Son, and God the Holy Spirit, with whom we will enjoy fellowship forever.

"Heaven will be a place where the inhabitants will be free from fears and insecurities that plague the present life. There will be no energy crisis; we will be free from the economic and financial pressure that oppresses so much of the earth. We will be free from fear of personal failure, and we will enjoy the social order that we have dreamed of finding for so long. There will be no night, death, illness, tears, ignorance, confusion, or war. Heaven will be full of happiness, adoration, love, and perfection. Our relationship will be intimate and direct with the one who made the heavens and the Earth, our Father Celestial."

---

### Revelation 21:2-5

*"Then I, John, saw the holy city, New Jerusalem, coming down out of heaven from God, prepared as a bride adorned for her husband. And I heard a loud voice from heaven saying, "Behold, the tabernacle of God is with men, and He will dwell with them, and they shall be His people. God Himself will be with them and be their God. And God will wipe away every tear from their eyes; there shall be no more death, nor sorrow, nor crying. There shall be no more pain, for the former things have passed away. Then He who sat on the throne said, "Behold, I make all things new." And He said to me, "Write, for these words are true and faithful."*

### *The Total Rescue*

Due to an act of God, brokenness, and necessity, I finally gave my life to the Lord, as I have already narrated in the previous chapters'; meaning that I gave the Lord power and authority to rule my life. I chose to do it as an act of humility and Faith whereby, with His immense power, He could take full control of my world. Both my husband and I recognized our need for a savior, a healer, and a restorer. We both realized that we needed to heal our emotional wounds and our interpersonal and social relationships because the world, life, and our many bad decisions had hit us hard, naturally and spiritually. We were at a point in our lives where we needed God the Father to lift our heads, heal our wounds, and come to us with all his love and power. He responded without delay. We understood that it was time to get to know Him up close and allow Him to act according to the design He had for us, exercising His great power to fulfill it.

We decided to remove the limitations we had placed on Him and His design or purpose for us, due to our limited knowledge and understanding. We started to see the light of Christ shine in our lives, and our world changed. Even our faces had a bright demeanor that others noticed. In the process, as the darkness that had invaded us was dissipating, His Light shone to illuminate the path for us to continue, and His right hand of justice sustained us. His Word says in John 14:6: I **am the way, the truth, and the life**. No one comes to **the** Father except through me.

The Book of Jeremiah, 3:33 says: "Cry to me, and I will answer you, and I will teach you great and hidden things that you do not know." So, believing in Him, we cried out and He responded. Our lives began to change radically, and His peace came upon us.

My husband, who at that time had recognized that he had no control over alcohol, cried out to God asking for help to not depend on harmful substances, and at that moment he was set free. To this day, he does not need alcohol to anesthetize his pain because God not only completely removed the addiction, but He also instantly healed his heart. People who have had addiction problems to a toxic or harmful substance, which are not few these days, know very well that this is a real miracle of significant proportions.

John 15:5

*"I am the vine; you are the branches. He who abides in Me, and I in him, bears much fruit; for without Me you can do nothing."*

We both understood we had lived separated from the Father for too long and needed to depend on Him for everything. We began to let ourselves be taught by His Word, Sunday teachings, and above all, to listen to and learn to know His heart.

Now we base all our decisions on His good, pleasant, and perfect will for everyone as the Scriptures teach. We learned that God does not need to subtract from one person to add to another; He always produces winners. Each time he is invited, there will be blessings. This change resolved many of our conflicts, and peace began to reign in our home. Together, we face life from this new perspective in Christ Jesus. Little by little, our wounds began to heal, and we were able to forgo self-centeredness, the product of immaturity, where we had lived for so long. Now we seek to understand more than being understood, and we continually approach mentors who guide us in the transformational process.

Our Heavenly Father used people to guide us along the path that we should follow. We allowed mentors who, to this day, remain present in our lives, to teach and correct us so we continue growing. Twenty years have passed, and we are still in the process and will always be, as no one ever knows everything there is to learn. Now not only are we receiving but also imparting on to others what we have learned so that they too, could know Jesus and enjoy the abundant life that He has promised. We are restored and are part of the work of the Ministry of Christ.

The beautiful, although broken, glass vase that I saw in the dream when I gave my life to Christ has been repaired and is no longer broken or disposable but has been restored to become a useful vessel. Now, we walk immersed in the work and service of the Lord. We continue to learn and serve in the church. We have grown and matured, serving as pastors and teachers of the Word for several years. We know that nothing we receive is because we are good, but because His mercy is great. We present ourselves understanding that "not with an army, nor with might, but with His Holy Spirit" (Zechariah 4:6). Now, repentant for our sins, for our old way of life and our independence, we can approach the throne of Grace with confidence.

# Final Prayer

*God of our Lord Jesus Christ, the Father of glory, may give to you a spirit of wisdom and of revelation in the knowledge of Him. I pray that the eyes of your heart may be enlightened, so that you will know what the hope of His calling is, what are the riches of the glory of His inheritance in the saints, and what is the surpassing greatness of His power toward us who believe. These are in accordance with the working of the strength of His might which He brought about in Christ, when He raised Him from the dead and seated Him at His right hand in the heavenly places, far above all rule and authority and power and dominion, and every name that is named, not only in this age but also in the one to come.*

**Ephesians 1:17-21**

# References

Chapter 1 Apostle Dr. Maldonado, Guillermo (2012) The Glory of God. New Kensington, PA: Whitaker House.

Chapter 2. Apostle Dr. Maldonado, Guillermo. I Need a Father.

Canaan Ministries – The Rivers in the Garden of Eden.

Chapter 3  Dr. Monroe, Myles. Men with Purpose.

Chapter 4   Dr. Bradshaw, John (1990), Homecoming: Reclaiming and Healing your Inner Child. Bantam Books.

Chapter 5  Apostle Dr. Maldonado, Guillermo (2013) Kingdom of Power, How to Demonstrate it Here and Now. Whitaker House, New Kensington, PA. 15068.

Dr. Monroe, Myles. Rediscovering the Kingdom, Pg 35. Destiny Image Publishers, Inc.